PRAISE FOR VINCENT ZANDRI

<u>Scream Catcher</u>

"SensationaL...masterful...brilliant."
~*New York Post*

"My fear level rose with this Zandri novel like it hasn't done before.
Wondering what the killer had in store for Jude and seeing the
ending, well, this is one book that will be with me for a long time to
come!"
~Reviews by Molly

"I very highly recommend this book...It's a great crime drama that is
full of action and intense suspense, along with some great
twists...Vincent Zandri has become a huge name and just keeps
pouring out one best seller after another."
~*Life in Review*

"A thriller that has depth and substance, wickedness and
compassion."
~ *The Times-Union* (Albany)

"I also sat on the edge of my seat reading about Jude trying to stay
alive when he was thrown into one of those games...Add to that
having to disarm a bomb for good measure!"
~Telly Says

<u>Lost Grace</u>

"Lost Grace is a gripping psychological thriller that will keep you
riveted on the edge of your seat as you turn the pages."
~Jersey Girl Book Reviews

"This book is truly haunting and will stay with you long after you
have closed the covers."
~Beth C., Amazon 5-star review

<u>The Innocent</u>

"The action never wanes."
~*Fort Lauderdale Sun-Sentinal*

"Gritty, fast-paced, lyrical and haunting."
~Harlan Coben, bestselling author of *Six Years*

"Tough, stylish, heartbreaking."
~Don Winslow, bestselling author of *Savages*

The Shroud Key

(A Chase Baker Thriller #1)

VINCENT ZANDRI

Bear Media LLC 2016
4 Orchard Grove, Albany, NY 12204
http://www.vincentzandri.com

Cover design by Elder Lemon Art
Author Photo by Jessica Painter

ISBN-13: 978-0615972145
ISBN-10: 0615972144

Published in the United States of America

"...When they came to Jesus and saw that he was already dead, they did not break his legs, but one soldier thrust his lance into his side, and immediately blood and water flowed out."
~John 19, 33-34

"The most famous human being in all of history was a first century Jewish revolutionary."
~BBC Documentary

PROLOGUE

Florence, Italy
October 2012

"You stole my wife!"

That rather inflammatory accusation is lobbed from a fully grown man who, despite his God-given gender, is most definitely screaming like a girl. A high school math teacher, to be precise, who's attempted two back-to-back roundhouse swipes at me and whiffed miserably.

"I did not steal your wife," I insist in as calm and unthreatening a voice as I can possibly muster under the circumstances. "Your wife stole me. Get it?"

Here's the deal:

I'm standing outside the Duomo Cathedral in beautiful, scenic Florence, Italy. No, that's not right. I'm not standing. More like I'm dancing, dodging the punches and swipes of this paunchy, Dunkin Donut fed middle-aged American. The American wants me dead. Dead and buried. Yet I feel terrible for him. His chubby face has gone heart-attack red, eyes swollen with tears and rage. His horrified wife looks on as do a crowd of tourists who have come to the Duomo to witness some glorious Renaissance history but instead have managed to acquire free ringside seats to a brawl between a walking tour guide and one very jealous husband.

How did I get here? How did guiding these nice mid-western white-bread Americans result in my pulling the rope-a-dope inside one of the most sacred piazzas in the world while in the distance the polizia alarms blare, and the crowds of Japanese gawkers look on in smiley faced astonishment?

The sad truth of the matter is this:

I did it by being me. Chase Baker, former sandhog turned bestselling thriller writer, slash private investigator, slash tour guide, slash full-time screw up when it comes to some of the more attractive female clientele.

So what harm can come from a little innocent flirting?

Just ask the man desperately taking swings at me, trying to knock my teeth down my throat.

Maybe this isn't the first time easy love has come my way via a tour client, and this isn't the first time a jealous husband has wanted to hurt me over it. It's just that this is the first time things have gotten physical in public, with potential clients looking on. So then, like a freshly dug grave that's caving in on all sides, I suddenly find myself way in over my head.

But then, this rather sensitive situation is not entirely my fault. For example, it's not my fault that the woman in question rang my doorbell at midnight last night, waking me from out of a sound sleep just to "chat" and drink a little Chianti together. Not my fault that I'm still the same not-entirely-worse-for-wear Renaissance man I was the day my now ex-wife walked out on me holding my infant daughter in her arms, shouting, "You don't want a marriage! All you want is a plane ticket to anywhere but here!"

What is my fault, is my having answered the door for this exceptionally attractive tourist in the first place. Better that I simply rolled over and ignored the ringing doorbell. Better that I shut out the image of her lush blonde hair, jade green eyes and legs so long and firm they began at her feet and ended somewhere inside her shoulders. Better that I reminded myself of her marriage status and then simply dozed cozily back to sleep.

But, of course, what made things worse is that the lovely tourist woke the dog. And once Lulu, your two-year-old black and white pit bull is awake, half the residents on the Via Guelfa are awake from her barking and carrying on.

Dragging myself out of bed, I ran my hands over my short hair and down my scruffy face. I stretched myself one way and then the other, feeling the solid muscles in my back and arms tense up. Opening the shutters onto the cool spring night, I felt the cool air touch my naked skin, and I laid eyes upon the blonde apparition thumbing my buzzer.

"It's midnight, Mrs. Doyle," I said out the open window. "I'm closed for business."

In the background, I could make out the noise of some revelers returning from the bars near the Piazza Del Duomo, their boot heels slapping against the cobble-covered roads.

"I just want to chat," she said, smiling, her alcohol-soaked voice sounding sultry and sexy in the night. In her right hand she gripped a five Euro

bottle of Chianti which she raised as an enticement, like she required an enticement with those eyes and everything that went with those eyes. "Look, Chase. I brought refreshments."

I felt my heart beating. Felt my blood flowing through my veins. I glanced down at Lulu who was standing just a couple of feet away on the smooth wood floor of my five-hundred-year-old third-floor apartment.

"What should I do, Lu?" I whispered.

"You know what you should do," the pit bull said with a wag of her tail. "You should go the hell back to bed. Get up bright and early in the morning, work on your new book, then get in a quick run before having to meet your group at ten for the Duomo tour. That's what you should do. Don't forget, you need the dough-ray-mi."

"Yah," I agreed, gazing back down onto the blonde *goddess dressed in short black mini-skirt, black lace tights and knee-length leather boots. "I should go back to bed, shouldn't I?"*

"But you're not going to do that are you, Chase?" Lu added. "As usual you're gonna listen to your dick, unlock the door for this lonely but very married tourist, invite her into your world. You're gonna drink her wine until it's almost gone and then you're gonna get naked. From that point on I gotta be forced to listen to your moans and groans and bed-board banging when I should be getting my rest. But then, what the hell do I know? I'm just a stupid dog. I don't even know I'm alive."

"You sure you're just a dog, Lu?"

"If it looks like a dog, smells like a dog, barks

like a dog..."

"*Most dogs don't talk human speak.*"

"*Most dogs ain't gotta live with you, Chase. And you're making all this dialogue up in your head anyway.*"

"*Thanks for reminding me, Lu. Thought I finally lost it for a minute.*"

Working up a grin, I inhaled a deep, satisfying breath, and decided, "What the hell?"

That's when I proceeded to jump down into the rabbit hole.

"*Okay, Mrs. Doyle, I'm gonna let you in. But just for an hour. Long day tomorrow, remember? The Duomo tour and the 'David' in the Academia. You're paying me big bucks for this.*"

"*Oh, good one, Chase.*" *Lu, moaning under her breath. "Real smooth.*"

"*Back off, Lu. Daddy's got a date.*" *A wide smile plastered on my face, I sprinted out of the bedroom to the front door. Unbolting the door, I leaped down the stairs to let her in...*

...Ten hours, thirty-three minutes, and sixteen seconds later, I find myself wrestling. Only I'm not naked and the person I'm wrestling with is most definitely not a jade-eyed blonde *beauty. I'm grappling with the overweight husband of said jade-eyed beauty.*

A one, Mr. Robert Doyle.

"*I knew you were with her last night when I rolled over and she was gone,*" *screams the red-faced faced man, as he tries to trap me in a bear hug. "I knew it the moment you set eyes on her you'd try and get in her pants.*"

I shove the far softer Doyle away, hold up my hands in surrender like I want no part of fighting him. And I don't. He's my client after all, and by the looks of his physical constitution, only two heartbeats away from a major coronary.

"She came to me, Mr. Doyle. Last night at midnight when I was asleep."

"That supposed to make me feel better, Chase Baker?"

In the near distance, the wailing sirens growing louder. So is the crowd that surrounds me.

"Fight!" someone barks. An Australian. "Don't just dance like a couple of Sallies."

Australians love to fight.

"Yah, punch his lights outs!" someone else shouts. A Japanese man. Sounds like, "Punch his whites out!"

But I really don't want to go all Russell Crowe on this man; don't want to punch his lights out. He's just angry, confused and hurt.

Doyle takes another swing at me, and another. This time he connects with my right jaw, sending a shock wave of pain into my head. It also flicks a trigger. My defensive trigger. The one that brings out Chase Baker the Survivor. The one that's been triggered in bars and Irish pubs the world over. Istanbul, Athens, Cairo, Rome. You name it. I've tossed my fair share of punches and swallowed a few too. But this is the first time it's happened while working.

"Chase, don't you dare hurt my husband!" cries the suddenly concerned voice of Mrs. Doyle. She's still looking mighty choice in her black mini skirt

and leather boots. She did her share of screaming last night in my apartment. Now she's screaming once more. Only difference is, she's changed her tune entirely. Her eyes are filled with tears and she's clutching her face with her pretty little hands. I'm the bad guy now. Like last night's little midnight affair was all my idea.

"Don't you dare hurt my husband you big bully!"

Her face is a combination remorse, fear and hatred for herself over what she's done.

I know the look all too well. I've seen that face before on a dozen other too-attractive-for-their-own-good girls whose husbands have just discovered the worst thing they can possibly imagine: That their pretty little trophy wives are also pretty little cheats.

My head is ringing like the Duomo bell. I feel slightly out of balance. So much so that I don't see yet another punch coming. This one connects with my other jaw. The crowd roars in approval.

If the first wallop triggered a survival mechanism, this one sparks rage.

"Sorry, Mr. Doyle," I say, "but you leave me little choice."

Taking a step into the bigger man's body, I lead with an uppercut that travels through the math teacher's soft underbelly all the way to his spine. I then quickly follow up with a left hook to the lower jaw and just like that, it's lights out for Mr. Doyle on the cobblestones of a breathtaking Renaissance treasure.

It's also precisely when the polizia arrive.

They jump out of their white and blue Fiat squad car, grab me by my weight-trained arms, demand that I drop to my knees. How's the old saying go? It's not the angry man who punches first who gets caught. It's the sucker who punches last who eats the crap sandwich.

"Hey, he started it!" I shout. But what I really should be doing is pointing at Mrs. Doyle, insisting, She started it!

The polizia don't want to hear it anyway. This isn't the first time they've picked me up for brawling and it certainly won't be the last. They push my arms up over my head in the opposite way God intended for them to be pushed. The pain causes little flashes of white light to explode in my brain as I feel the steel cuffs being slapped over my wrists.

"You big bully!" shouts Mrs. Doyle as she slaps me across the face. Then, dropping to her knees over her out-cold husband, "Oh my sweet darling, are you okay?"

"Let's go, Chase," one of the blue-uniformed cops insists in his Italian-accented English. "You've got yourself a front row audience with Detective Cipriani...Vai, vai."

"Does this mean I'm under arrest, officer?" I say as they painfully yank me up onto my feet.

"Si," the other cop says. "It means your ass is glass."

"Grass," I say. "It's 'ass is grass.' Why don't you learn to get it right, Pinocchio?"

I feel the quick fist to the gut, and it's all I can do not to double over.

"Why don't you learn to shut up, Chase?" the cop says. "Silencio."

"Good idea," I say through gritting teeth. "I should learn to shut up and you should learn to speak English...The international language of choice the world over."

Together the cops drag me to the squad car where they thrust me into the back seat, slamming the door closed. An EMT van arrives on the scene then, the medical technicians immediately exiting the vehicle and going to work on the still prone Doyle. Meanwhile, the cops hop back into the front of the cruiser.

As the cop behind the wheel pulls away from the piazza, I catch one more glimpse of Mrs. Doyle. She's still kneeling over her husband. I shoot her a smile, like, Thanks for last night. But she returns my glance with a glare that would ice over Dante's Inferno. When she raises up her right hand and flips me a manicured middle finger, I realize I should have listened to my dog, Lu, and not my other head.

"I'll never learn," I whisper to yourself. "Oh well, at least Detective Cipriani has nice cigars."

I contemplate smoking a fine Cuban cigar all the way to polizia headquarters.

1

"Signor Chase Baker!" shouts the guard sergeant as he approaches the iron bars of this dark, dank, basement holding cell. "You are free to go! Andare!"

I shove through a pen that's filled mostly with drunk, piss-soaked vagrants who've migrated from Peru. Why they cross over the big drink to Italy instead of heading north to America, which is far closer, beats the hell out of me. Maybe they get better health care here. Or maybe it has something to do with a higher alcohol content in the beer...Yeah that's it, more alcohol in the beer.

The barred door slides open.

I step on through, offer the uniformed guard sergeant a smile like, *Top o' the mornin' to ya!* Or, *Top o' the late afternoon anyway.* He doesn't smile back. Go figure.

"Su," he says, nodding at the staircase before me.

Su...That's Italian for "up." As in, *Get the hell up those stairs!* It's also something an American redneck might shout at an old dog before kicking it in the ass with his Redwing-booted foot.

"Up the stairs, Chase. Detective Cipriani would like a word with you in his office."

"He asking or telling?" I say.

But the short, stocky cop just glares at me like he has no idea how to answer my query. And he doesn't. The guard sergeant on my heels, I climb the concrete steps as ordered, like an old dog being led around by his master.

A minute later I'm granted my private audience with Florence's top cop. If you want to call him that. Detective Federico Cipriani closes the door to his office, asks me to take a seat in a wood chair set before his long dark wood desk. Set out on the desktop is a translucent plastic baggy that contains my personals: my belt, the laces to my boots, my wallet, my passport, my cell phone, my cigs, my Saint Christopher's medal, my gun, my bullets ... I go to reach for them.

"Not yet!" barks Cipriani, from across the room. "We need to talk first, Chase."

I sit back, my eyes peeled on the internationally licensed 9 mm Smith & Wesson.

"Looks like the Doyles aren't pressing charges," I say. "How sweet of them."

The fifty-something Cipriani goes behind his desk, sits himself down. He's a big man with a barrel chest and a pleasant looking face mostly hidden behind a thick but well-trimmed beard. His eyes are brown as is his hair, and the dark blue suit he wears was no doubt purchased in Florence, probably at the department store across the street from the Piazza Della Republica.

"It's true they have dropped their case of assault against you," he nods, picking up my handgun, staring down contemplatively at it. "But that doesn't excuse you from punching the merda out of an American tourist."

"You detaining me further, Cip?" I say, pronouncing the nickname like "Chip."

He shakes his head.

"No, just trying to somehow get it through that thick skull of yours that the time will come when I can no longer keep you out of trouble. Eventually you will be asked to leave Italy for good."

I force my eyes wide open.

"Never," I say. "Who will guide all those lovely lost women who've just arrived from America and England and Australia and Japan and China and Russia and…?"

"I'll never understand it why a bestselling author like you still insists on providing guided tours or working as a private detective or even a, what do you call it, sand dog? Doesn't make sense."

"Three reasons," I say, slipping my hand inside my bush jacket for my cigarettes, but then quickly realizing that they are stuffed into the plastic bag along with my lighter and my bullets. Oh well, I've been trying to quit on and off for years now. "One, writing is a solitary existence. It gets mighty lonely. Second, guiding, detecting and sand*hogging*—not sanddogging—provides me with badly needed human contact and it also makes for good story material now and again. Third, the money is good and on occasion great. Royalties are good too but not always so consistent. You with me here, Cip? Just think of me as a Renaissance man living and thriving in the home of the Renaissance."

He spins the gun on his thick index finger like a little boy and his plastic six-shooter, bites down on his lip.

"You know I don't like that you are able to carry this in my peaceful town of art and culture."

"Money talks," I smile. "Especially in Italy. Just ask the American GIs who saved your ass from Nazi enslavement during World War Two. And you personally signed off on my permit, don't forget. Besides, this isn't your town anyway, Cip. It's Brunelleschi's town, or haven't you noticed that big giant marble dome occupying the center of the city?"

"You're not getting any younger, Chase. Soon you will not be so attractive to the young women who travel to this beautiful country. Perhaps you will now consider spending more time with your daughter in New York City." Working up a smile. "You know, grow old gracefully. With dignity."

"The food is better here. So is the wine. And I'm forty something. I'm not even close to old, yet."

Cip sets the gun down on top of his desk. Opening the small wooden box set beside it, he pulls out a cigar, cuts the tip off with a small metal device he produces from his jacket pocket and gently sets it between his front upper and bottom teeth. Firing the cigar up with a silver-plated Zippo, he sensually releases a cloud of blue smoke through puckered lips. Then, slowly straightening himself up in his swivel chair, he reaches across the desk with his free hand, pushes the box of cigars in my direction.

"Thought you'd never ask," I say.

Stealing a cigar from the box, I bite off the tip, spit it onto the wood floor. Leaning over the desk, I allow the cop to light me up.

"You always were a class act, Cip," I say, sitting back. "When do I get my gun back?"

"Not yet," he says. "I have a favor to ask of you first."

I exhale the good tasting and very smooth Cuban-born smoke. If silence were golden, we'd be bathing in the stuff.

Finally, I say, "Okay, Cip, you've got that look on your face like we're going to be working together again whether I like it or not. What do you need? You want me to dig up some dirt on someone? Maybe follow some cheating hubby around Flo for a while?"

He shakes his head, smokes.

"Not exactly," he explains. "But you're right. It's possible I have a job for you."

"I'm listening, so long as it pays."

He gets up, comes around the desk, approaches the set of French windows behind me, opens them onto the noises of the old city.

"I need you to find a missing man for me," he says after a time.

I turn in my seat, looking at his backside as he faces out onto the cobbled street below.

"Find him where?" I say, knowing the question sounds like a silly one since if Cip knew where the man was he wouldn't be asking me to find him in the first place. But it's a good place to start.

"Somewhere in the Middle East would be my best guess. Egypt, perhaps."

I smoke a little, visions of my sandhogging days in and around the Giza Plateau pulsing in my brain.

"Egypt," I repeat. "Not the safest of places at this point in modern global history."

"Especially if you're an American. And the man I want you to find is indeed an American."

"What's his name?"

Cip backs away from the window, returns to his desk. Only instead of reclaiming his place behind it, he takes a seat on the desk's edge, left foot dangling off the edge, the right foot planted.

"His name is Dr. Andre Manion. A biblical archeology professor from a small Catholic college in your Midwest. An expert on the historical Jesus of Nazareth and said to have discovered some relics belonging to the Jesus family."

The name strikes home. So much so that a lesser man would allow the small electrical shock of the name to show on his face. But I'm not a lesser man. Or so I pretend.

"Did you say relics? Jesus relics?"

"Yes I did. Priceless antiquities, which no doubt stir your juices, perhaps more than Mr. Doyle's wife did last evening. Manion's over here on a teaching sabbatical at the American University. Or supposed to be here teaching, I should say. Early last month he went missing and hasn't been seen or heard from since."

Cip is right. The name Manion when combined with relics and antiquities does indeed stir my juices.

"Fact of the matter is this, Cip: I worked as a sandhog for Manion eight years ago in and around Giza where we were in search of some prized Biblical treasures. Perhaps the most prized Biblical treasure of all. But we never did find much of anything, and truth is, Manion ran out on me, leaving me hopelessly hungover and alone."

"Sounds very dramatic, Chase," Cip smiles. "I thank you for your honesty."

"Don't mention it. Obviously my life has improved in leaps and bounds since those days."

"Obviously," Cip says. "That prize fight performance in the Piazza Del Duomo is proof of that."

"Very funny," I say. Then, "Thought you said Manion was in Egypt?"

"That's the best possible guess based upon what we've put together thus far. I didn't say there weren't any clues as to his specific whereabouts inside the embattled country. I said he himself hasn't been seen, other than on airport security video in both the Florence and Cairo airports."

"He traveling alone?"

"Don't know the answer to that."

"Exactly what relics has Manion uncovered?"

I feel my heart race as I ask the question.

"Don't know the answer to that either," he admits. "But I've heard a rumor that he uncovered the small tomb that housed the bones of Joseph,

Jesus's father. But that was a while ago now and in any case, finds of this magnitude would naturally be snatched up by the Vatican. That is, the finds can be verified in the first place. Naturally you would be familiar with such a process."

"Naturally," I say. "Or at the very least, the relics would go to the highest bidding private collector. Perhaps someone from Moscow. Or maybe one of your richer-than-God friends in Florence, Cip."

The top cop smokes, glares at me for a moment, like he's waiting for the stink from my comment to dissipate.

I add, "I assume your support staff has done everything in their power to locate him?"

"And then some. We've even gotten Interpol involved. But they, too, have come up short. Egypt is not the most cooperative of countries since its revolution and the election of a radical Islamist-backed government."

I reach into the right-hand pocket of my bush jacket, pull out a small notebook and a Bic ballpoint that Short, Stocky Guard Sergeant failed to relieve me of before tossing me into the pen with the drunk Peruvians. I click on the back of the pen with my thumb, jot down the name Manion, as if I need to. Then I write the name, Jesus, as if I need to do that also. Finally I scribble in a dollar sign, just for good measure. Makes me smile when I look at it.

"Manion got a wife? A mother? A boyfriend? Someone I can speak with who might help me out here?"

I can't recall if the professor was married at the time we were digging all over Egypt. I recall him mentioning a woman now and again. But I don't recall her name.

"His wife is in town. She teaches English at the same college her husband teaches at. She's been here for a couple of weeks now. She desperately wants to find him. In the meantime, she can be a wealth of information for you, if you play her the right way and keep your dick in your pants."

"Hey, you know me," I smile.

"That's what I'm afraid of."

"Who would I be working for? You or her?"

"If you take the job, you'll be working directly for her. She's independently wealthy I'm told."

"My kind of client."

He slides off his desk, goes around it to his top drawer, which he pulls open. He slides out a manila envelope and tosses it across the desk so that it lands on the desk's edge. I take the package in hand and go to open it when he stops me.

"Take it home," he insists. "Examine it. Take your time. You should know that this one won't be easy. It will also be dangerous."

"You mean I can actually say no for a change?"

"Sure you can, Chase. Under one condition."

"And that is?"

"You pack up and head back home to the states, since I will personally revoke your temporary work permit and your permit to carry a firearm in Italy."

"Those are my choices?"

"Take them or leave them."

I smoke and pretend to think about taking the job.

"Can you perhaps give me a hint about what it is

Manion was working on and why he was willing to disappear in order to find it?"

But then, I already know precisely what he's working on. I just want to hear it from the good detective's smoky mouth.

"My guess is that Manion is being paid by a private investor to locate something of extreme sensitivity in religious circles."

"Which means it would be worth a lot of money in people circles," I say, my eyes no doubt, lit up like the lights on a Christmas tree.

"Watch yourself, Chase," Cip warns. "If what Manion is in search of is as important as I think it is, more than one person will be willing to die in order to get their hands on it."

I feel the weight of the package in my hands.

"What the hell is Manion after, Cip?"

I need to hear it, to believe it...

Exhaling, he says, "I don't know for sure since you will have to speak to his wife. But it's possible that the professor has stumbled upon something that is liable to shake up the very foundation of Christian belief as the world knows it."

The words aren't exactly what I want to hear, but on the other hand, the words can only mean one thing. I stand up, my head feeling a little lightheaded from the cigar and from what Cip is telling me.

"And that is?" I press.

"The bones of Jesus himself."

There, he said it. Said what I wanted him to say.

For the love of God, the quest for the mortal remains of Jesus begins again.

2

I grew up with Jesus. The product of a Catholic school guarded by yard-stick wielding nuns who could make the toughest of corrections officers look namby-pamby, I grew up fearing the big guy. My mother and father might have feared him too, but they were nonetheless devoutly, overtly and hopelessly Catholic.

My father, at one time, considered becoming a priest. But I think he knew deep inside he could never be married to a faith, despite its impenetrable strength. A faith could never bear children, for instance. No way faith could bring in the big bucks like excavation contracting and sandhogging all over the globe could. So, instead of donning a stiff white collar and a black suit, my dad operated a backhoe, managed a shoveling crew, and he made money.

My mother bore me and two older sisters whom I no longer kept in touch with once our parents were dead, buried, and seated beside the Lord they so revered. I don't think of my family all too often. Try not to dwell on where I came from and how I made my way out of its confines. But I do sometimes find myself thinking of Jesus ... The historical Jesus of Nazareth.

I have no doubt that he once existed. That he must have been a great man and a powerful presence for him to be remembered so precisely, with such reverence and acclaim. Religions have been created in his name and many wars have been fought over his beliefs or, the beliefs mortal man have attributed to him. I fought in two of those wars in both Iraq and in Afghanistan. The wars were about the control of oil, but they were also about radical Muslims versus Judeo/Christians.

As I walk back towards my apartment across the Piazza Santa Maria Novella, I picture the long-haired man of legend being lashed by Roman soldiers while down on his knees, a crown of sharp thorns piercing his forehead, the blood streaking down an anguished face. I picture him walking the narrow cobbled streets of Jerusalem, a heavy cross bearing down upon his shoulder, he dropping to his knees under the heavy burden. I picture him being nailed to that cross on an ugly rock-strewn quarry called Golgotha or Skull Place and which is located just outside the city walls, the cross being raised slowly by the scarlet-robed soldiers, until the heavy vertical beam dropped down in place, his body falling hard against the nails that pierced both flesh and bone.

Is it possible that Manion is finally on the true trail of the Jesus Remains?

Walking the cobbled streets of a Medieval city filled with churches and cathedrals honoring Jesus's name, I can help but imagine the enormous sum of cash the true bones of Christ would fetch on the private collector's market. If Rupert Murdoch is willing to pay $100 million for the bones of Richard III, might he not be willing to scrounge up $500 million or even a billion for the remains of the Son of Man?

Listen, I might get hot and bothered by the thought of digging up that kind of relic, but I firmly believe they belong in a museum to be studied and pondered by scholars for eons to come. However, I wouldn't be averse from taking a few million for my efforts should I happen to come upon them during my search for Manion.

Why?

Bestselling author or not, the truth of the matter is this: My finances are in a shambles. As of late, neither my books nor any one of my other occupations are making me any money. As for sandhogging, that job dried up eight years ago in the hot Giza sand when Manion ditched me for a plane back to the U.S. I don't live in Florence because I love it. I live there because the lease on my downtown Manhattan apartment is about to be terminated due to unpaid rents.

You might also recall Detective Cipriani mentioning the fact that I have a daughter. That's right. Chase Baker, free spirit, bon vivant, and all-around Renaissance man is a dad.

Maybe finding adventures and writing fictions based upon them has become a passion for me. But my eight-year-old, long brunette-haired, brown-eyed daughter, Ava, is the love of my life. Problem is, I've fallen so far behind on the support payments that no way I can fly to the states and not expect to be slapped with an injunction as soon as I get off the plane. If I'm ever to see my little baby again, I'll have to make good on all my debts before I leave Italian soil. That means a substantial, if not huge, payday.

Perhaps having stumbled onto the job of finding Manion is the best luck I've had in a long time. That in mind, I climb the stone stairs to my apartment, knowing that gripped in my hand is not just a packet of information about an archeology professor who's gone missing in the pursuit of Jesus.

It just might also be my ticket back home.

My ticket back to Ava.

3

Lulu greets me as soon as I come through the door. Which tells me she's snuck into the main apartment from her bed out on the terracotta-covered terrace via the open window that accesses the dining room. My fault for leaving it open. The small but muscle-bound dog jumps and yelps until I pick her solid body up in my arms and hold her for a minute or two. Then, letting her back down, I make up a bowl of the dry dog food she eats for breakfast, lunch and dinner, and set it onto the kitchen floor. I grab a cold Moretti beer from the fridge and sit down at a breakfast counter that abuts a set of tall French doors leading out onto the grape vine-covered terrace.

Opening the package, I slide out the materials it contains. Not much in the way of information. A couple of eight-by-ten color glossies of Manion.

He's the man I remember. Tall, salt and pepper-haired, professorial-looking. His long face is clean shaven, his cheeks sunken in a bit, lips thin and uninteresting, as are his eyes which are brown and neither large nor deeply set.

If I didn't already know that he is an archeologist I would peg him for an accountant, or maybe a department store manager. In the photo he's teaching a class, his right hand extended up at a blackboard upon which a diagram has been drawn. If I have to guess, the diagram represents a crypt of some kind. An ancient, ornate burial chamber. I've seen the real thing plenty of times before.

In the second photo, the professor is shown working an archeology dig. I can't be sure, but it looks like he's in Israel. I've dug in the Jewish state on several occasions and I recognize the unique way the sun shines down on that porous, almost hospital white rock. In the photo, the tall, gawky Manion is wearing khaki clothing and a baseball hat with cloth flaps hanging down from it in order to protect the exposed skin on his neck. If I remember correctly, the world-class archeologist has a problem with sunburn. Being of Mediterranean descent, the hot sun doesn't bother me. Even equatorial sun. It just makes me bronze. My good luck. Good luck for the ladies too.

Setting the photos back down, I grab the vital stat sheet Cip provided for me which is typed out on Florence Polizia letterhead.

Manion, Andre, PhD—Archaeology/Psychology, University of Chicago, 1982, University of Chicago, 1984

Height: 6'1"
Color: Caucasian.
DOB: Feb 23, 1964
Status: Separated/Divorced

I set the paper back down.

"So check this out, Lu," I say. "Manion isn't just an archeologist. He's also a shrink. Funny combination. Never knew that about him."

Lu looks up at me from her food dish.

"Who's Manion?"

"Oh, I forgot to tell you. Manion is our meal ticket home. He's apparently gone missing in the desert. Probably outside Cairo where he's working on digging up the bones of Jesus and who knows what else. I worked with him once before, until he ran out on the dig and me."

"Jesus ... You mean the Jesus Died-On-The-Cross-For-Our-Sins Christ?"

"The one and only. What's important is that if I find Manion, I just might get a chance at digging up a few treasures of my own. Or perhaps even assisting in acquiring the very relic Manion is looking for. What a payday that would bring in my canine friend."

Lu coughs something up into her mouth, then swallows whatever it is.

"Isn't that stealing?" she asks.

"No. Errr, yes. But not like stealing in the classical sense. If those unearthed relics are truly up for grabs then it's first come, first serve. That's the law of the desert and the law of tomb raiding. But I am a little confused about one thing: the Professor Manion I once knew would never think of selling out to a private collector. But, from the looks of it, somebody's financing his new dig and that somebody has enough money to not only lure him away from his teaching gig in Florence, but also to simply render himself legally missing."

"Sounds dangerous. Jesus is one important human."

"In human terms, perhaps the most important man who ever lived."

"Then it stands to reason that if this Manion guy is about to locate his mortal body, a lot of people are going to want to have at it. Maybe even be willing to kill for it. You still got a gun, Chase?"

I drink some beer, pat my left rib cage upon which hangs my newly liberated 9 mm.

"As always, Lu."

"Where you gonna start looking?"

"Not sure. I need to speak to Manion's estranged wife first since she's the one financing the search. Word up is she's in town already. So, I guess you could say my search starts right here in Flo."

"Be careful, and remember, you're talking to a dog here."

"Thanks Lu. I trust you won't tell anyone about our conversations."

"That would be up to you since you're the one making this shit up."

"Duly noted."

The last items contained in the package are several newspaper clippings.

The first one is lifted from the *New York Times* and it's dated February, 2002. It shows Manion standing before what I immediately recognize as an ossuary, which is nothing more than a square shaped box carved out of sandstone. It's about the size of a banker's box and the lid is gable-shaped. The headline on the piece reads, **Bones of Jesus' Stepfather Found?**

The article describes the controversial discovery of a box on the Israel side of the Sinai which supposedly contains the bones of Joseph, Jesus's father and husband to the Virgin Mary. The article states that the ossuary has been carbon dated back to the early first century and contains both Aramaic and Latin text of the time. According to Manion, the inscription of the box reads, "Here lies the body of Joseph, father of Jesus and James, husband of Mary." Naysayers, however, say that the bones could belong to anyone since the names Joseph, Mary, James, and even Jesus, were very common in those days.

"I guess the court is still out on that one," I whisper to myself. "But then, how many men actually had sons named Jesus and James while being married to a Mary, way back in first century Palestine? Couldn't have been all that many."

I'm still contemplating the Joseph ossuary when my doorbell rings.

Setting down the article, I slide off the stool, head out of the kitchen, through the dining room which also serves as my writing room. Past the library and its bookshelves, and relic-covered walls, past the living room and its high, wood-beamed ceiling and finally to the stone-covered vestibule.

Unlocking the deadbolt, I open the wood door to a woman. A tall, very well built woman of maybe forty, with short light brown hair and deep blue eyes. She's wearing a black turtleneck sweater, black jeans and black, lace-up boots. She's also wearing a matching leather jacket. Strapped over her shoulder is a bag, also made of leather, and perhaps purchased in the Florence leather markets. The kind of bag I might store a manuscript in.

"Mr. Chase Baker?" she says, her eyes wide, her bottom lip trembling just slightly. "I hope I'm not intruding."

I have to force myself to peel my eyes off of her. But me, being me, it isn't easy.

"Can I help you with something, lady? I'm working."

Lu scrambles up beside me, pressing her muscular body against my shin. She growls which catches me a bit by surprise. Lu usually loves people. Even strangers.

"It's okay, Lu," I say.

The woman catches sight of the pit bull, takes a tentative step back. She tries working up a smile. But it's obvious the dog is making her uncomfortable. Or maybe it's me who's making her nervous.

She says, "I thought Detective Cipriani would have told you I was coming?"

I shake my head.

"Must have slipped his mind. Who are you and what are you doing on my doorstep?"

"Do you always act this tough?"

"Only around beautiful women who come calling unannounced."

"Maybe I should introduce myself," she says,

reaching out and gently touching my arm. "I'm Mrs. Andre Manion. It's my husband who's gone missing."

I stare down at her hand.

"Your husband?"

"Correction," she exhales, gently retreating her hand. "Ex-husband."

"So I hear," I say, still playing it cool despite her luscious eyes. "And what would you like me to do about it?"

"I want you to find him."

"And then what?"

"Bring him back alive," she says.

4

She enters into the apartment, her shoulder brushing against mine as she walks past. Setting her bag on the couch, she gives the place the once over.

"Looks like a museum," she laughs. Then, turning to me, "If you're making coffee, I'd love some."

"Is that an order?" I say, playing hard to get. "Because if it is, I haven't agreed to taking on this job. Looks dangerous enough for me to lose my skin. And I like my skin. It fits nice."

By all appearances she has no idea about my history with her husband, and that's the way I want to keep it, at least for the moment. If she knows I went after the Jesus bones with him once before and he had cause to run out on me, no way in hell will she tolerate me getting a second chance to make a grab for them. She'll just assume I'm some sort of opportunistic grave robber looking to make a quick buck. And the hell of it is, she'd be right.

"That's not your reputation, Mr. Chase Baker," she says. "I'm told you are quite handy around an archeology dig and even handier when it comes to finding a missing person. Both in real life and in your novels."

"You've read my books." It's a question.

"All three of them. *Deception* was my favorite. I loved how the detective deciphered clues only by looking at their reflection in a special handheld mirror. Clever. Even your prose was passable. I teach English, you know."

"The mirror was the book's hook, Ms. English Prof."

"Indeed and it's a good one. It's almost like you took it from real life."

"Maybe I did. But how do I know you're not just trying to butter me up here?"

She cocks her head, which admittedly, is a very pretty head, then bites down gently on her bottom lip.

"I have no reason to compliment you on your work. If I want something from you, I will ask you directly."

"So why not just ask me politely to help you find your husband?"

She smiles.

"I already have, and so has the detective. I've just come to confirm the status of your employment."

The room falls silent on us, on the many books, on the many pieces of treasure I've accumulated over the years in Europe, the Middle East, South America and God knows where else. Skulls, amulets, statuettes, rocks, jars of ashes, and a mirror. A special mirror about the size of a credit card and almost as thin. A mirror that's broken in half and that I dug up inside a deep pit outside the Third Pyramid within the Giza Plateau back when I was sandhogging for Manion ... But that's only for me to know.

"Think I'll make some coffee," I say, heading into the kitchen.

Pulling down the stove-top coffee pot from the shelf over the sink, I fill the bottom with tap water, and the coffee receptacle with Lavazza espresso. I light the gas stove, set the pot on the burner and wait for the magic to happen. When it does three minutes later, I pour the coffee into an espresso cup, grab hold of my already open beer, and carry them back out to the living room.

I find her standing, facing my floor-to-ceiling shelves, gazing upon the books and relics.

"You have quite the collection," she says. "You remind me of the most interesting man in the world...a real Renaissance man."

"I've heard a lot of women call me a lot of things. But never that." I hand her the coffee. Then, "So, Mrs. Manion, remind me of your given name again."

She turns to me, carefully sipping her coffee.

"My first name," she says. "It's Anya."

"Anya and Andre," I say. "How cute."

"We were a cute couple. Very much in love. A long, long time ago."

"Now you are divorcing. Or already divorced."

She nods, sadly.

"My husband has been carrying on an affair for a long time, Mr. Chase—"

"—Just Chase."

"Thank you, Renaissance man, Chase Baker ... Anyway, my husband has been carrying on an affair that has become his obsession."

"I'm sorry to hear that," I say, visions of the many women who have come through this door over the years, their husbands still waiting for them unawares back in their hotel room. "Seems like nothing is sacred when it comes to marriage these days."

She shakes her head vehemently.

"You don't understand," she adds. "If my husband were to have an affair with another woman, that would be one thing. We might be able to work that out, and start over. But this one is different."

"I'm not following," I say, taking a swig of beer.

She sips her coffee, comes up for air.

"My husband is not carrying on an affair with a woman."

"Oh, I'm sorry," I say. "He's switched teams."

"No," she laughs. "I could deal easily enough with that too."

"Okay, Anya, let's have it. Who is your missing husband seeing behind your back?"

She finishes her coffee, sets the cup down onto the wood coffee table, straightens up, crossing her arms over her chest.

"He's carrying on an affair with Jesus," she says.

"And that's why I've left him."

I finish my beer, go grab another one, take it back with me into the living room.

"Let me get this straight," I say. "You left your husband because he's overly obsessed with finding the bones of Jesus. Yet here you are standing in my living room asking me to find him? Why not just let him go and get on with his obsession? Live your life? Teach your English classes?"

Her face takes on a pained expression. Like the coffee I just served her is making her sick. She gently sits herself down onto the couch.

"I didn't say I don't love Andre, Chase," she says. "Love *and* care about him. All I said is that our marriage is over."

"But you still want me to find him for you?"

"I'm worried about him. About his ... let's say health."

"Why not leave it to the police? To Interpol? Doesn't make sense to pay me when they can do it for free."

Me, still playing hard to get. To perhaps up my price. Maybe considerably so.

"No," she says. "I would prefer to keep the police out of the loop as much as possible. Andre's work is very sensitive."

"So are the people he's working for, no doubt."

She stares at the wood plank floor.

"Yes," she says. "It's possible that if the police were to become involved by making themselves plainly visible, grave harm could come to my husband."

"Better to hire me and put my head on the

chopping block," I say. "I don't come cheap. Neither does my head."

She says nothing for a heavily weighted moment. Just as well. I use the time to drink a little more beer. It's while drinking the beer that it hits me. Professor Manion didn't just get up one morning, get dressed, head to the airport and fly away on his own. He had a little help in the matter.

"Anya," I say. "Is it possible your husband was kidnaped?"

She looks at me hard. Not at me, but into me.

"It's not only possible, Renaissance Man," she sighs. "It's the sad truth."

5

"I'm gonna come clean," I say, straightening out the shoulder strap on my black, Tough Traveler writing satchel. "I know your husband. Or, used to know him. I worked as a sandhog for him eight years ago in the Giza Plateau."

"I had no idea," she says, shooting me a look of suspicion. But I'm listening to my insides and they are telling me she could be putting on an act. "Why did you wait until now to tell me?"

"I didn't want you to think I'm some opportunist who wants to find your husband only to ultimately find the treasure he's no doubt seeking."

She works up a grin that makes me want to press my lips against hers. But not yet.

"Seems strange you not knowing about my past relationship with your husband," I say, recalling my conversation with Cipriani. "You just happen to call on the one man in all of Florence to try and find your husband and it turns out I'm very familiar with him."

"Stranger things have happened, Renaissance Man," she says, brushing back her lush hair with her hands. "Do you still want the job?"

"Give me the rest of the truth," I say, shifting the weight of my satchel over my shoulder. "Straight, no bullshit."

The apartment has grown too cramped, too tense. What I want is for Anya to tell me everything about her husband … everything I don't already know, that is … and do so over a drink at a nice quiet bar down the road in the less touristy Via Guelfa, American University area not far from where Manion was supposed to be teaching. It's precisely why I've put Lu back outside on the terrace and locked up the apartment.

Now walking side by side on the cobbled Via Guelfa, Anya goes on with her story: "My husband has been researching the remains of Jesus and his family for years. Most people, including scholars thought him crazy. Because even if the remains somehow exist, it's likely they would never be found. The desert, even around the Giza plateau, is just too massive. Or perhaps they've already been found and now reside in a secret chamber in the Vatican. Or perhaps they have turned to dust like so many ancient bones. But then Andre found the Joseph remains, and the world took notice. So did the church. From there on in, the greater possibility that Christ's bones could be found, took on a greater reality."

I'm aware of most of this. It was what attracted me to Andre in the first place in the early years of the new century. Not only his knowledge about the possible resting place of the Jesus remains, but his utter belief in their existence.

Up ahead is the DaVinci Bar. The exposed brick building is mostly frequented by art students and professors drinking coffee and smoking cigarettes. It's also quiet, dark and cavernous enough that we can talk in privacy while fading into the far shadows.

We enter and take a table in back. Setting my satchel onto the table, I go to the bar, retrieve us both a glass of vino rosso a piece. I bring the wine back with me to the table, set it down and sit across from her.

"But I thought the Joseph bones were found to be frauds," I say, continuing where we left off. "You telling me the Joseph bones were real?"

"The Vatican did it's best to debunk them," she says. "And the media sided with the Pope. But Andre knew different. He knew he was on the trail of finding Jesus now that he had Joseph's bones and evidence of a Jesus family crypt outside the Jerusalem walls. He was also gathering the attention of some pretty serious investors, which made him nervous, of course."

"Such as?"

"One man in particular. A wealthy Egyptian from Cairo and a friend of their new, rather radical President."

"What's his name?"

"That's just it. I don't know his name because he

never would tell me. Something about the less I knew the healthier it would be for the both of us. But I do know this: The wealthy man is an oil tycoon by trade and in the possession of infinite resources."

"Do you think it's possible he is the one who kidnaped Andre?"

She sips her wine. Nods.

"You have to ask? The wealthy man is no doubt a part of the Muslim Brotherhood which worked so hard to push their party into absolute power after a revolution which promised freedom."

"I don't get it," I say. "Why would a Muslim be interested in Jesus?"

"Power," she says. "The ultimate act of crushing the Roman Catholic Church and tipping western belief onto its side."

I steal a sip of wine. I also take a look over my right shoulder at the small crowd gathered around the half dozen tables that fill the place. At one of the tables near the front entrance sits a solitary man. Not an unusual situation for this place. A dark-haired man, with a salt and pepper beard, black leather coat, reading glasses. He's gazing at a newspaper. *The Florentine.* Florence's English newspaper. Probably a professor, if I had to guess. No doubt from the same school where Andre was teaching before his abduction.

I turn back to Anya.

"I'm still not making the connection between the bones of Christ and the Muslim Brotherhood, other than their tremendous monetary value to the right investor."

She straightens herself up, runs her hand through her thick hair.

"Don't you see, Chase?" she says. "Islam reveres Jesus. They believe him to be a great miracle maker. The Koran speaks almost as highly of Jesus as they do Mohamed. But they also believe in something that the Vatican would rather we not know about."

"And that is?"

"They believe that the man crucified on the cross somewhere around 30 AD was not Jesus, but a double. A fill-in if you will. They believe that the disciples protected the real Jesus and slipped him out of Jerusalem to protect him from his enemies."

"The Jewish Sanhedrin and the Romans."

"Once he was condemned and put to death, the movement Jesus started would be over. That's the way the Sanhedrin and the Romans saw it anyway. That way they could maintain their way of life. All self-proclaimed Messiahs were dealt with this way. But, Jesus of Nazareth was different. He wasn't a quack screaming his head off about doom's day. He was the real deal."

"A real threat, in other words."

I feel something cold run up and down my spine. It's the same ugly feeling I would often experience eight years ago when I first accompanied Andre in search of the mortal Jesus. I knew then, as I know now, that you don't undertake a task like that lightly. I also glance once more at the man reading the paper. He's staring at us in between glances of all the news that's fit to print.

I add, "I'm beginning to see why this wealthy

Egyptian, whatever his name is, would be so interested in acquiring the bones. If they are proven to belong to the historical Jesus and if it's also proven that he was not crucified but lived to be an old man, it would inevitably show that the Koran is right and the Bible is wrong."

"It would empower the Muslim Brotherhood and perhaps even factions like Al Qaeda like never before and it would effectively destroy the foundation upon which the Catholic Church has been established."

"How badly does this wealthy man want these bones?"

"Very badly. Enough to kidnap my husband and do so under Egyptian government authority."

I drink some more wine, look once more at the man. He's staring back at us. I pull a ten Euro note from my pocket, set it down onto the table, slide it under the empty glass.

"Let's go," I say under my breath.

"I haven't finished my wine," she says, looking up at me with those stunning pools.

"You're finished. We're not safe."

Gazing over her shoulder, she says, "That man is staring at us."

"There's a toilet in back. There's also a door that leads to the outside right beside it. Go now. I'll be right behind you."

She hesitates.

"Go. Now."

She gets up, walks to the rear of the bar.

I wait a full minute, then get up, grab my satchel, tossing the strap over my shoulder, and follow. I

haven't yet reached the back door before I make out
the heavy footsteps of a man running after me.

6

Anya is standing outside the door, her face a patina of panic and confusion.

The door is solid wood and locks from the inside, but swings open onto the outside. Behind us exists a sort of gravel-covered, fenced-in no man's land which surrounds two small, blue plastic and metal dumpsters. One for refuse and another for recyclables. There's some concrete blocks and some two-by-fours set beside the dumpster.

The door opener rattles and begins to open. I push it shut with my arm and shoulder.

"Grab that two-by-four," I bark.

She does it.

I take hold of it with my left hand, jam one end into the gravel, then shove the other end under the brass closer. Pulling myself away from the door, I search for a way out of that small yard.

"This won't hold for more than a few seconds," I say, taking her hand.

"Where will we go?"

The man behind the door might have been following Anya for a while now. He might have followed her to my apartment earlier. In fact, it's very likely he followed her.

Behind us in the near distance, the ugly gray walls of the American University. A short chain link fence separates us from the school grounds.

"Your husband was teaching at the university. I assume they gave him the use of an office?"

"Yes," she says.

The man is pounding on the door, the two-by-four about to give way.

"Now's the time to show me."

She looks over her shoulder at the university building.

"This way," she says, and together we make our way over the fence and to the school.

The American University was built back in the 1960s. It is as uninteresting and sterile as the rest of Florence is beautiful, historic, and inspiring. Anya leads us through throngs of young students to a multi-storied concrete building marked "Science and Science Labs." Entry to the facility requires a key-code which you must punch into the keypad set right beside the metal and glass door.

"I don't know the code," Anya confesses.

"Just wait a moment," I say, shifting myself to the side of the door. "Someone will come along. In the meantime, keep an eye out for the man in black."

We wait for a beat or two, all the while, my eyes shifting from the door, to Anya, to the road behind me. When a man and a woman emerge from the door, the two of them engaged in deep academic conversation, I take hold of Anya's hand and slip us both inside.

"Slick," she says, as we enter into the wide open vestibule.

"What did you expect from a guy named Chase?" I say, smiling.

"Guess this means you're officially working for me … Ren Man," she says as we approach the elevator.

"What the hell is Ren Man?"

"Short for Renaissance Man," she says. "That's a mouth full. Ren Man just rolls off the tongue a hell of a lot easier."

"You sure you want me to work for you?" I say. "You haven't heard my rates yet. What floor?"

"Second," she says. "Whatever the rates are, I'll pay them."

I hit the button containing a light-up arrow that points towards heaven.

"I'm beginning to like you, Mrs. Manion," I say, recalling how my dog Lu growled at her. "Even if I do suspect you're nothing but trouble."

"You have no idea, Ren Man," she says, smiling wryly as a bell chimes and the doors to the elevator slide open.

7

The office of Dr. Andre Manion is located midway down a brightly lit concrete corridor on the right-hand side. When I grip the opener, I find that it's locked. No surprise there. I step back from the door, look over one shoulder, then the other. Mounted to the exterior walls just inches below the concrete panel ceiling is a series of security cameras.

"Don't look now but we're being filmed," I point out.

Anya cocks her head over her shoulder.

"We are most definitely *not* being filmed," she says. "Those cameras are decoys meant to look like the place is secure. From what I'm told the American University constantly runs in the red."

"How do you know all this stuff if you and the missing hubby are split up?"

"First thing Detective Cipriani did when he found out my hubby, as you call him, was missing was to check the university security surveillance film. Stood to reason that if my husband simply walked out of here or worse, that he was kidnaped right out of his office, than it would be caught on film." She sighs. "Sadly, no such film exists since these cameras are for show only."

"What about a video of him leaving through the front door? Those cameras have got to be real."

She shakes her head.

"They're real enough," she says. "But no Andre to be seen on film."

"Then he was picked up off the street," I add. "Or maybe outside his apartment. Cipriani claims to have seen video of the professor at both the Florence and Cairo airports."

"Maybe. But what difference does it make at this point, Chase?"

She's got a point. This isn't a criminal investigation I'm running here. It's a rescue…More or less.

Reaching into the interior pocket on my worn leather bomber, I grab hold of a twenty-some-year-old Swiss Army knife. A gift from my dad before I disembarked for the first Gulf War back in '91. "Keep this where you can get at it quickly," he whispered into my ear before kissing my cheek and pressing his face against mine. I remember feeling the wetness of his tears as I stepped onto the Amtrak train that would take me to New York City and JFK, not wanting to look back into his big weeping eyes and risk seeing him like that. People die in wars. Young people. What if that was the last time we would ever see one another in this life?

Using the fingernail on my index finger, I pull out the metal pick option and slip it through the narrow hole located in the center of the closer. By pushing and twisting the pick, I feel the spring release on the closer's locking mechanism. With my free hand, I twist it counter- clockwise. With a pleasing metal-separating-from-metal snap, it opens.

"We're in," I say, opening the door wide.

I step in and Anya follows, closing the door behind her.

"Lights," I say.

I hear her fumbling against the wall for a switch.

"Got it, Chase."

The room fills with bright white lamp light, thanks to the ceiling-mounted fixtures. The small, cramped, square office is filled with cardboard boxes that rest up against the wall to my right while to my left, numerous volumes occupy a steel bookshelf. Directly ahead of me, a metal desk is covered with scattered papers and photos.

I go to the desk and immediately see that maybe a half dozen eight-by-ten color glossies have been placed on top of a map. At closer inspection I can see that it's a map of Egypt. The Giza Plateau in particular. I slide the map out from under the pictures. It's covered in scribblings made in red Sharpie. So many lines, circles, and nonsensical doodles that I can't begin to make sense of it.

The photographs however leave nothing to interpretation. They are representations of the same

49

white-on-black, photographic negative-like image.

"The Shroud of Turin," I whisper aloud.

"The Jesus burial cloth," Anya confirms, stepping beside, so close I can feel her leather-covered shoulder rubbing up against my own. Her touch, no matter how slight, doesn't feel unpleasant. "Another one of my husband's obsessions."

I scan the photos which, too, are veined in red marker, as if Manion were searching for something he was convinced must be contained in the shroud, but not quite seeing it yet.

A map...He was looking for a map. Or a blueprint...

There are full body shots, head shots, arm and leg blow ups, even a zoom in on Christ's apparently blood-soaked hair.

"Question," I say, turning to Anya, hoping to squeeze a little more information out of her. "Why would a man concerned with looking for Christ's bones waste his time studying a crusade era forgery?"

She looks me in the eyes.

"It's true the shroud was finally proven beyond a doubt that it dates back to 1352. That the pigment covering the cloth is not blood but paint. Vermillion and madder to be precise."

I was a bit struck by her obvious knowledge of the shroud. But then, I could only guess that she was able to pick up quite a lot about her husband's work by living with him for all those years.

"My question stands then. Why study it at all?"

"Because the shroud is more than a depiction of the body of Jesus as he was laid to rest in the tomb of Joseph of Arimathea immediately following the crucifixion. Andre was convinced that it was a giant map which was created in order to keep a precise and running record of the Jesus remains locations."

"Locations?" I ask. "As in the plural usage?"

"Yes, take it from a Freshman English Comp 101 teacher...Location*ssss*." She exaggerates the s at the end of "locations" making it sound like an extended Z.

I feel the light hairs on the back of my neck stand up at attention. Feel my blood begin to flow faster. So Andre had been onto something all along. Eight years ago whenever he'd bring up the subject of the shroud and its map-like possibilities, I would laugh and shrug it off as a nutty professor's overactive imagination. But now it appears his theory had some real validity to it.

She goes on, "For centuries people have been trying to make sense of the shroud, wishing and praying that it was the true cloth that wrapped Jesus's remains when he was pulled down from the cross. Proof of the mortal corpus *and* the divine resurrection incarnate. But in all their zeal to confirm their faith, they never stopped for a second to consider that the shroud could actually be a guide in disguise. A way for the disciples, the bloodline of the disciples, and eventually, Holy Roman Catholic Church to keep track of the Jesus remains once he died."

"The cloth has been guarded over by Franciscan monks for centuries," I point out.

Anya nods.

She says, "The Vatican only allows limited

testing every twenty years and even then by a handful of scientists they hand pick. For the rest of the time it's locked in an impenetrable vault. It's not even available for public display in its bullet-proof glass case expect for once every dozen years."

"Why give something that much protection if in essence it's just another 14th-century painting that might be hung in the Uffizi or the Louvre?"

"Precisely because the Vatican is aware of its true meaning as a map. A purpose and a meaning that would disprove the essence of Christianity."

"A purpose shrouded in the form of a fake image undergoing a false transformation." I burst out laughing. "A brilliant deception. The shroud is really the ultimate proof of Christ's mortality while at the same time masquerading as ultimate proof of his divinity. Talk about sheep in a wolf's clothing."

"Andre knows all this of course, and for years he's been begging the Vatican for close inspection of the shroud. It's part of the reason for his coming to Florence to teach within the proximity of the shroud in the first place. If he could get a serious look at it, he might discover not one map of the present whereabouts of the Jesus remains, but many maps detailing many different resting places. Andre firmly believed the bones were always on the move because they were always being hunted."

"Like now," I say. "He must have the map hidden somewhere."

"No," she says, once more shaking her head. "There's one major problem with my husband's map theory."

"And that is?"

"Whoever created the shroud wasn't foolish enough to simply draw detailed maps on the back and front of the Christ image. They hid them somewhere within the body itself. Existing photographs haven't been helping Andre find a precise location. They only offer tidbits of information. He needed to see the entire thing, face to face, in real-time."

"So you're telling me Andre never actually uncovered a precise map." It's a question.

"Portions…Suggestions, but not a full map. A few lines and squiggles which were most definitely added in recent decades that, in this case, match up to specific locations in the Giza Plateau. While these recent map-like additions rule out previous locations or any other location for that matter, they still only spoke to Andre in generalizations." Raising up her hand, pointing at the map. "Thus the photos and the map occupying the same desk."

"This tells me two things," I say. "First: Your husband only knows the *approximate* location of the burial site. And two: The people who kidnaped him have yet to steal the goods."

Wide-eyed, she nods.

"It might also mean that while the bones are still out there awaiting discovery, Andre is still alive."

"Yes, they will need him alive if they have any hope in unearthing their precious bony relics."

A bump on the office door. Not like a knock or a kick with the foot. More like someone, or something, trying to get in.

"Lock the door the door," I say.

Anya immediately jumps over to the door, locks

the closer. That's when whoever is on the other side begins twisting the opener. Hard.

The man in black...

"What do we do, Chase?"

I grab up the photos, stuff them in my satchel. I fold up the Giza Plateau map and stuff that too into the satchel. Giving the room a scan, I look for a way out.

"There's no windows," Anya says.

"I'm well aware of that," I say, looking for something, anything that will provide us quick egress.

Then I see the HVAC diffuser mounted to the top of the concrete block wall. Neither Anya nor myself are particularly big people. It might be a tight fit, but we just might be able to slide ourselves through the duct and down into the next room.

The person on the other side of the door is yanking on the closer, the door violently slapping against the metal frame. I pick up the desk chair, position it under the wall-mounted duct. Stepping onto the chair, I once more pull out the Swiss Army knife, this time fingering out the blade. Using the tip, I break off the heads of the old screws, then pull out the grill, dropping it to the floor.

"You first," I say, jumping down from the chair.

"Through there?"

"Yeah, this always works in the movies."

For the first time since I've known her, Anya truly smiles. She steps up onto the chair, sticks her head and shoulders into the duct.

"A little help please," she says.

I place one hand on her firm butt while wrapping

my right arm around her legs.

"Pleasures all mine," I say, heaving.

"For a Ren Man, you're a real pig, Chase Baker," she says, before disappearing into the darkness.

8

I'm right behind her.

I drop down into the next room onto my black booted feet just as I make out the sound of Manion's office door being kicked in. We're standing in the dark inside someone's office. An office that appears to be empty, if not for an odor. Not a foul odor but a pleasant one. Aftershave maybe. Like Old Spice. Stuff my old man used to splash on his face before church on Sunday. I'm picturing the face of my old man when the body hits me like I've somehow stepped in front of a speeding truck. I go tumbling back against the wall.

"Chase," Anya screams.

"Find a light switch," I shout.

The man who tackled me led with his shoulder. The classic football tackle. He might have even bruised a rib. But he's not quick in retreating. I grab him in a headlock with my left arm while with my right, pull my automatic from its shoulder holster. I press the business end of the pistol against his skull.

"Don't shoot," comes a voice. The voice of an older man. He speaks English, but the accent is most definitely German.

I release him.

The overhead light comes on revealing my attacker. He's a short, gray-haired and bearded man dressed sloppily in an old wool blazer and corduroy pants. Most definitely a professor. He's even got a plastic pocket protector filled with pens and pencils plus a translucent six-inch ruler.

"I thought you were a burglar," he says, panting. "Or perhaps, a rapist."

"You've got some spunk, Einstein, I'll give you that. We're the good guys. The bad guys are on the other side of this wall. Think you can call security for us?"

His eyes light up. He glances at my gun.

"I haven't had this much fun since I earned my PhD in Physics forty years ago," he smiles.

"We're going to leave now," I say, crossing the office and joining Anya at the door.

"Go, go," the professor insists, picking up the phone on his desk, punching in a number. "I'm calling security. In the meantime, if they come through that vent, I'll be waiting for them." He raises up his free arm and makes a muscle under his jacket sleeve. Like I said, he's got some spunk.

"Sorry for the intrusion," I say.

"No worries. You made my day."

He begins speaking into the phone in Italian. I

take hold of the door opener, slowly twist the knob, pull the door open, poke my head outside into the hall. I look both ways for a man dressed entirely in black.

"All clear," I say. "We'll take the stairs."

"Roger that, Chase."

"Roger that?"

Holding her hand, we step out into the hall, and take it double-time all the way to the stairwell.

Down on the first floor, we head back out into the street.

People surround us on all sides. Students mostly, carrying books, canvases, sketchpads, knapsacks. Always moving about in pairs or groups. They stare at us with curiosity and perhaps even a little fear as they pass.

I grab Anya by the shoulders.

"We need to get back to my apartment while our tail is still busy upstairs with security. After that we'll have to find another place to hold up. The apartment isn't safe anymore now that I know you're being followed."

"I'm sorry. I just had no way of knowing."

"Don't be sorry. Goes with the territory. Sad thing is, that man probably isn't the only one watching you." Removing my hands. "Let's move."

"I'm right on your ass," she smiles.

"Now who's the pig, Anya Manion?" I say.

We run.

9

The door to my apartment is open.

Correction, the door has been jimmied open.

"Stay here," I say, turning to Anya. "Whoever did this could still be inside."

"Not on your life, Ren Man," she says, following me into the vestibule.

Reaching into my bomber, I pull out my 9 mm, thumb off the safety. Taking a slow second step into the vestibule, I move on into the living room, scanning it with the gun barrel. I then head on across the dining room and into the kitchen. Both appear to be empty. Opening the door onto the terrace, I can see that no one is hiding out there either.

"Lu," I say, not loud, but loud enough for the pit bull to hear me.

That's when I hear the noise coming from the

other side of the apartment.

"Bedroom?" Anya says. It's both a statement and a question.

I run from the kitchen to the vestibule just as he's coming out the bedroom door. A big man, dressed in dark clothes. He raises up an automatic, aims the business end for the center of my chest. Pointblank.

I stop.

The shot from his gun echoes throughout the apartment, the bullet nicking the wood beam over my head. Sucking in a breath, I lower my aim, depress the trigger, and shoot his left leg out from under him.

The search for Andre and Jesus has just gone nuclear.

Both Anya and I go to the big wounded man, where he lies on the stone, vestibule floor.

"Grab his gun," I say.

She does it.

I drop down onto one knee, press my still smoking barrel against his forehead.

"Who do you work for?"

He's clutching at his bleeding leg.

"Go to hell," he says, his accent distinctly Italian.

I cock back the hammer.

"Una volta," I shout. "One more time … Who sent you?"

"One more time," he says through grinding teeth. "Go. To. Hell."

I slide the barrel away from his forehead, press it against the thigh on his healthy leg.

"No!" he screams through gritting, grinding

teeth. "Please."

"Tell me … Now."

He swallows his pain, tries to suck down a breath.

"I am a holy man," he whispers. "If you want to know who sent me, look no further than divine providence. I am a messenger of God."

Slowly, I stand, turn to Anya.

"The Vatican," I say. "He's a soldier of the Vatican."

"What do we do with him?" begs Anya.

She's standing over him, looking panicked and pale in the face. Chalk white against her black clothing.

"We leave him."

"He could die. Bleed out."

I grab hold of her arm, look her in the eyes.

"Since you came through my door an hour ago, lady, I've been chased, been made to crawl through an air diffuser, tackled by a little old man, shot at and cursed to hell by some man who claims to be on God's side. Now my dog is missing. You want me to find your husband, you do as I say."

Her eyes well up. I can tell she wants to say something, but she just can't work up the words.

I release her arm.

"My apologies," I say. "But you're turning out to be a boat load of trouble, and if we are somehow able to survive these next few hours, the sooner we get out of town the better."

"Why don't you just stop?" she cries. "Don't work for me if I'm so much trouble."

She wipes a tear from her eyes.

"Because I'm already in too deep. I know what you know and they'll come after me, regardless of what I do." But on the inside, what I'm telling myself is this: I'm not leaving for U.S. soil without those holy bones.

She smiles against the tears. But, as if reading my mind, she says, "Okay, the job is still yours for the taking. But I have to ask you, is it really my husband you want to find, or is it a fortune in Biblical treasure?"

Releasing a breath, I find myself nodding. Maybe she's right. Maybe what I'm after besides some much-needed money is fortune, glory, and immortality. But not even fame holds a brightly lit candle to the possibility of once more being close to my daughter.

I turn away from her, head into the bedroom. After a fruitless search for Lu in all the obvious places, including under the bed, I go to the safe which is built into the far wall. Opening the safe, I pull out three extra ammo mags which I stuff into the left-hand pocket of my bomber. Reaching into the safe again, I grab a plastic sandwich baggy containing several SIM cards. I also grab my passport, plus three wads of Euros. Each rubber-banded wad is worth 5,000 Euros a piece. I step out into the hall, and hand her one of the cash wads.

"What's this?" she says, her tears now dried up.

"That's a loan," I say. "I can only assume you don't have much on you."

"We're not going back to my hotel room?"

"We're not going to Andre's apartment either. It's too late for that. They'll be waiting for us there too. That's what I would do anyway if I were them."

"Who's *they*?"

"The Vatican soldiers, and who the hell knows who else."

"Where will we go?"

"Let's hope you have your passport on you at all times like a responsible traveler should."

Reaching into the interior pocket on her leather jacket, she produces her passport and her wallet.

"Plenty of credit cards," she smiles, like this is her way of contributing to the cause.

"Can't use 'em," I say. "They'll track us if we use credit cards." Then, "Where's your cell phone?"

She digs into another pocket, pulls out an I-Phone.

"Shit," I say, taking the phone in hand. "Was hoping you had a Droid. You could use one of my SIM cards."

Dropping the phone I stamp on it, and crush it with my boot heel.

"Hey!" she barks. "That phone cost me a grand back in the states."

"Sorry," I say. "It might be a fancy phone but it's also a tracking device. How do you think they been tailing you so easily?"

Her eyes go wide.

"What about your phone?" she says.

I hold up the sandwich baggy.

"SIM cards. Makes my phone like new again every time I change one out."

The Vatican soldier on the floor is moaning in pain, blood pooling around his leg.

"I need to grab something else," I say. "In the meantime, go through his pockets, see what you can find. Then we have to leave this place. It's too damned hot."

"What about your dog?"

"I'm guessing the man of God took a shot at her and missed. Otherwise her blood would be all over the place. Instead she took off running through the open window. She's probably in Pisa by now."

I approach the bookcases while Anya searches the semi-conscious Vatican soldier. Scanning the books beginning with H, I pull out one of the many antique copies of the Holy Bible I possess. I open the book. There's a square cut-out in the center of the pages. I made the cut-out myself. Inside it is stored a small piece of mirror I dug up while sandhogging for Andre in the Giza Plateau eight years ago.

I pull out the mirror, feel the solid weight of it in my hands. Feel its ancient construction and revel in its mystery. I stare down at my reflection in the flat, gold-rimmed surface. I stare into my brown eyes, and I see my father. He was a digger, like me. But he possessed a special, spiritual gift.

Once, when he was hired to excavate a foundation for a new office building, he suddenly killed the power on the machine, mid-scoop. He jumped down from the cockpit, screaming at everyone to move away from the site as quickly as their legs would take them.

Those were the days before electronic finding devices. Before smartphone apps that tell you where buried cables and gas lines are located. While the diggers who worked for him all ran for cover, my dad slowly made his way to where his big, sharp-toothed, dinosaur-like scoop barely touched the raw soil. He reached into his pocket, pulled out his pocket knife. Flipping up the long blade, he then gently stabbed at the raw earth. The blade didn't enter the dirt and clay for more than an inch or two before he struck cast iron. That cast iron belonged to a far too shallow gas main that, had my dad pierced it with his backhoe, would have blown the entire site to Kingdom Come and my dad right along with it.

Developing a sixth sense for what might come your way ... for buried pipes, electrical lines and even buried bodies ... It was a gift my dad developed or perhaps was born with. A gift from God, maybe. But it was something he tried with all his might to instill in me. Some might refer to this gift as simply "going with your gut." But for me, it's more than that. It's like learning to believe in the invisible. I guess it isn't all that different from faith. Believing in something you can't see, touch, or feel, but somehow knowing it exists all the same. Knowing it exists as sure as the blue blood that flows through your veins.

Returning the Bible to the bookshelf, I clutch the small, three thousand-year-old mirror in my hand, well aware that the voice in my gut wants me to bring this along for the ride. That at some point, I am going to need it. For what exactly and when, I have no idea. But I know that when the time comes, it will be there for me.

Pocketing the mirror in the right-hand pocket of

my tan Levis, I go to Anya.

She looks up at me from where she's kneeling on the floor.

"Nothing," she says, shaking her head. "He's got nothing on him. Not a scrap of paper."

"Most pros won't carry anything, just in case something like this happens to them."

The man is down on his back now, mumbling something in his semi-conscious state.

"What's he trying to say?" Anya says.

"You mind?" I say.

She scoots back while I drop down onto my knees, position my ear near his mouth.

He mumbles, "Erastus ... Erastus ... Erastus ..."

I straighten up.

"What's he saying?" Anya asks.

"Don't know," I say. "Sounds like the name, Erastus, to me. But who, or what, the hell is Erastus?"

"Maybe he's speaking another language."

"God only knows. But what I do know is that we need to get out of here and I don't want him bleeding out on my floor any longer than he has too."

Anya stands.

"Go now," I say. "Out the front door."

I stand, listening to the man mumble, "Erastus" with his desperately wide eyes.

She steps out the door and begins making her way down the stairs to the landing. I give the Vatican soldier one last look. It's then I notice, resting on his chest, half hidden by his black button down shirt, a small wood and gold cross. Kneeling once more, I pull the cross out from under the shirt. Soldered to the vertical beam of the little Maltese cross is a woman. An angel. Or perhaps Mary, the mother of Christ. It's a beautiful amulet that I have no intention of stealing. But there it is again: That feeling in my gut. The one my dad helped instill. Dad and who knows, maybe God Himself.

Yanking the cross and its leather strap over the Holy thug's head, I pocket it along with my mirror, and leave my Florence apartment. Perhaps for the final time.

10

At the bottom of the landing, my gun gripped in my left hand, I open the front door, stick my head out like a rabbit peeking out of its hole. Look both ways down and up the Via Guelfa. No one in either direction. No one who appears to be an immediate threat anyway.

But this ancient street is bordered on both sides by four and five-story brick and plaster buildings with shuttered windows every few feet. The street fighting here during World War Two was ferocious since it was so easy to hide and find cover behind those five hundred-year-old walls. If you were caught by the enemy alone and unprotected in the street unawares, you were dead.

I take Anya by the hand, lead her out onto the street. Just a couple of sitting ducks looking for a safe haven.

"Where are we going?" she begs, as I re-holster my gun and as she pulls her hand from mine. "I'm not a child."

"Good, that means I don't have to treat you like one."

"Go to hell, Chase."

"I'd have to die first. And I'm doing my best to prevent you from causing that to happen."

"Told you, you can quit anytime you want."

"And I told you I'm already in too deep. Just ask that Vatican asshole bleeding all over my vestibule floor."

"I'm sure if there wasn't a substantial amount of money in this for you, you'd be quit by now."

I turn to her, smile.

"Money sings. And I love music."

We round the corner onto the Via Nazionale, then negotiate our way through the throngs of tourists, natives, cars, trucks, and scooters until we come to Via Faenza. We hook a right at the corner gelato joint and cover maybe fifty meters over a winding cobble road before I stop outside a guesthouse called Il Ghiro. I depress the intercom button that's embedded into the stone wall beside the tall green door.

"Ciao," comes a tinny male voice. "Can I help you?"

"Checco," I say into the intercom. "It's me, Chase."

"Chase!" barks the voice. "Come stai?!"

"Friend of yours, Ren Man?" Anya says, not without sarcasm in her voice.

I shoot her a glance.

"A friend who will help us and just maybe save your life....My life...Your husband's life inevitably. He might even locate my dog for me." Looking her in the eye. "But he doesn't come cheap."

"I get it," she says. "But if you feel he's necessary."

Back at the intercom.

"I'm not so good right now, Checco," I say. "Need your help."

"Come up," he says. "Come, venire."

The old wood door opens with the loud mechanical release of its bolt.

"After you, precious," I say to Anya.

"At least you got one thing right," she says, stepping inside.

I follow, the door slamming like a prison gate behind us.

Set before us is a long corridor beset by cold plaster walls on both sides. There's a staircase at the very end.

"All the way up," I say. "Five floors."

Without a word, Anya begins her climb. So do I.

Checco is already waiting for us on the stone landing at the top of the stairs, illuminated in the late day sunlight that leaks in from the overhead skylight. He's a man in his mid-forties, taller than average height, but possessing the thin, wiry build of a marathon runner, which he is. His black hair is thinning and when he skips a day shaving, noticeable signs of salt begin to pop up out of his smooth cheeks along with the pepper. But his mannerisms, unstoppable optimism, and constant smile give away the perpetual boy inside of him. He is also one of the most expeditious fixers I know working this side of the Atlantic inside a guesthouse called Il Ghiro, but which is really just a front created by whatever organization or organizations he works for. And like I said, he doesn't come cheap.

Anya steps up on the landing beside me, and I can't help but notice Checco's eyes go wide. He takes her hand and, like David Niven would in some 1940's Hollywood production, kisses it.

"Enchanted," he says in his perfect, but accented, King's English.

Anya returns her smile, slowly lowers her hand.

"A real gentleman," she says, her eyes on me. "You might take a lesson from Checco, Ren Man."

I slap the Italian on the arm.

"Thanks for making me look bad."

"Nothing to it," Checco laughs. "You do a very good job of it on your own."

"We don't have a whole lot of time," I say, cutting to the chase.

"What is it precisely you need?" Checco asks.

"I'll tell you when we get inside. Preferably, over a couple of drinks."

"You both look like you could use more than a couple drinks," he says.

A half hour and two glasses of Chianti later, I've explained everything I know to Checco. I've told him about the missing professor and how Detective Cipriani personally handed me the case after threatening me with deportation. I also told him how Anya, Manion's estranged wife, showed up at my door a few hours ago and how we haven't had a moment of peace since, including a soldier of the Vatican making an attempt on our lives. I told him everything.

"Don't worry about your dog," Checco says, coming around to his desk inside the fifth-floor guest house office. "I promise you we will find her and bring her back here. But, before all else, we need to get that man out of your apartment before Detective Cipriani's officers in blue get to snooping."

"That is if his own people haven't already done it for him. Assuming he isn't working solo, that is."

"Very true," he says, logging onto his laptop computer. "Unfortunately it would not be a very good idea for you to head back there and make a check on the place. Too dangerous. I'll send one of my own men."

"Second thing?" I pose.

He smiles. "The Shroud," he says, as if reading my mind. "You want to get an up-front-and-personal visit with one of the most protected sacred relics in the Roman Catholic canon."

"Can it be done?"

Checco sits back in his swivel chair, cathedrals his fingers at the knuckles, rests them in his lap.

"It's possible," he nods. Then, smiling, "Do you recall my old girlfriend, Natalia?"

"From Moscow," I say, picturing a tall, beautifully built long-haired blonde woman of about thirty. "How could I forget her?"

"Boys," Anya whispers, crossing her arms over her chest.

"She is a curator for the shroud," he says. "I will call her. See what I can arrange. But no promises." He stands. "In the meantime, you need a place to rest and I need to gather up some transport tickets for you. Train and air. I'll need both your passports."

We hand them to him. He pulls a key from the drawer, comes around his desk.

"I only have one room available," he says, not without a grin. "I'm sorry."

"Suits me," I say, tossing him a wink.

"Spare me, Chase," Anya says. "You wouldn't know where to begin with me even if you had the chance."

11

Slipping off my bomber, I decide to leave my shoulder holster strapped to my chest. You never know what might come through the door when you least expect it. The prize at the end of this journey isn't cash. It isn't jewels. It isn't some ancient pottery dug up in and around the Giza pyramids. The prize is nothing other than Jesus of Nazareth whom some call God. God is within my grasp.

Startling thing is, I may be closer to the Jesus remains than even Andre, that is my intuition...my *gut*...is serving me well. All that stands between the bones and my hands, is the Shroud of Turin. Getting at the professor and getting him safely back will come too. But not before I'm certain of where the bones are hidden.

I pour myself another glass of wine, put my feet up on the bed. I lie back against the propped up pillow while Anya heads into the bathroom, starts the shower, gets undressed. I try not to think too hard about her getting naked. Best to keep it professional. At least for the time being.

Coming from outside the open window are the sounds and smells of this busy Tuscan city. People walking in both directions, the hard soles on their boots making a distinctive slap against cobbles that were laid hundreds of years before they were born and that will still be here hundreds of years after their death. After their children's children's deaths.

I sip the wine, feel the alcohol's calming affect. Then, pulling my smartphone from my pocket, I dial Detective Cipriani. He answers after two rings. I offer him a short update, minus the part about my plan to get my hands on the Jesus remains, if they do indeed exist, as soon as the job of finding Manion is finished.

"And you are safe for now?" he asks, in his raspy, but low-toned voice.

"I can only assume."

"Soon you will find Dr. Manion and you will be able to go home."

"I just want to see my daughter and not get arrested at the gate when I land in New York."

"Keep on doing the right thing, Chase, and you will see her very soon."

"You think so, huh, Cip? Appreciate you not pulling the plug on my resident status."

He laughs.

"I've never known you to be so polite, Chase. But thank you for trying. I'm certain you are not very pleased with me at present. But one hand washes the other, as they say, and right now, both our hands are dirty. Call me as soon as something new develops."

He hangs up at the same time the sound of running water coming from the shower stops. Sitting back on the bed, I know that Cip's use of the adjective "dirty" isn't indiscriminate. If he knows anything about the Jesus bones then I can only assume it's possible he wants something out of them too. In fact, perhaps it's even possible that he's not overly concerned about Manion, so much as he's interested in what prize Manion is after. Being a cop in Italy, where the prime minister openly carries on affairs with child prostitutes, is not the straightforward business it can be in the states. Chip might be a good cop, but he can also recognize an opportunity to make some good side cash when he sees it. I should know. I've gone after several would-be criminals on his behalf who weren't wanted for any crime in particular, other than they owed him money. The bones of Jesus ... should they happen to fall into his hands ... would most definitely constitute the chance to make some excellent side cash. Millions upon millions of dollars or Euros of side cash.

A couple of minutes later, Anya emerges from the bathroom. She's wearing only a white towel that barely covers her breasts and the top couple of inches of her smooth, milky thighs. Her brown hair is wet but neatly slicked back, her brown eyes wet, her lips thick and inviting. She pours herself a glass of wine, issues me a slight sideways glance as she goes to the window, opens the shutters wide, allowing the air to cool and dry her at the same time.

"What are you looking at, Ren Man?" she says while stealing a slow drink of wine.

I sit up, slide off the bed. Stepping up beside her, so close I can smell the heat coming off her naked skin, I take hold of her glass, set it down onto the window ledge. I take her in my arms, gently. She pretends to struggle, but not enough to tell me to back off.

"If you're trying to figure out a way to say thank you," I say, "it's okay. You don't have to."

She issues a quick laugh.

"Remember," she says, "you're being paid ... Paid well. You're doing me no favors."

Our eyes lock and I feel drawn into her. I sense she's feeling drawn into me also. With the window open, I can feel the cool air on my neck. I know she can feel it on her exposed shoulders. Moving in closer, I feel my mouth gravitating to hers and hers to mine. Our lips touch ...

... Then Checco barrels into the room.

"No time for love, Chase," he barks. "Time is wasting. If you want to see the shroud you have to leave now."

Anya quickly pulls away from me, as if we're back in junior high school and her parents have just arrived home unannounced.

Checco smiles, his brown eyes bright and shiny.

"Am I interrupting something? Perhaps I should leave."

"No, Checco," Anya says, making the towel

more tight and secure around her torso. "Chase and I were just enjoying the view outside the window … Isn't that right, Chase?"

"Couldn't have said it better," I exhale. "Just enjoying the view." Then, "What do you have for us, Checco?"

He reaches into his jacket pocket, produces a stack of tickets, our passports and also a new smartphone for Anya.

"Natalia and I have discussed the situation," he says. "She will grant you access to the shroud. But you must come immediately."

"How soon is immediately?" I say.

"Now." Looking at his watch. "The five-ten train to Milan and from there, you connect to Turin. Natalia will see you tonight at seven thirty outside the sacristy doors of St. John the Baptiste. You will be traveling together. But with an assumed identity." He disappears into his office down the hall. When he comes back he's holding a box in his hands. "The sizes might not be perfect, but they will have to do on such short notice."

He sets the box on the bed. I go to it, open it, lift out the first article of clothing.

A navy blue nun's veil.

I toss it to Anya.

"That is going to look damn good on you, Sister," I say.

"And this will look heavenly on you, Chase," Checco says, pulling something else out of the box.

It's a priest's collar.

"You have a plan to go with these getups, Checco?"

"Allow me to refresh your wine," he says, heading back out of the room, "and I will confess everything to you."

"Good choice of words," Anya adds.

"Get dressed, Sister," I say. "I'm having unholy thoughts."

"The shower's right in there," she says, cocking her head towards the bathroom.

"The cold water will do you wonders, padre."

12

For the time being, I've become a priest and my present employer, Anya Manion, has become a nun.

Dressed in black pants, matching jacket over a black shirt and stiff white collar, I am traveling under the assumed name of Father John Crews. Anya is playing the part of Sister Rosaire de Marie, and the navy blue nun habit she dons proves it. We are two ecumenical scholars studying the shroud and its history. Together we believe the fourteen-foot length of cotton fabric is not a medieval fake, but the true two thousand-year-old burial robe of Christ. That is, according to the documentation provided to us by Checco. The forged documentation signed and sealed by the Vatican and presently stored in my shoulder bag, along with fake passports, grants a private one hour viewing of the shroud, even though the sacred relic is presently unavailable for viewing by the public for at least another three years.

Now seated on the high-speed train, the Tuscan countryside speeding past, bathed in the orange glow of the spring dusk, I open the shoulder bag, pull out the shroud photos and the Egypt map I found in Manion's office. The first photo reveals the full shroud. The photo is really a negative image of the body imprinted on the cloth so that the crucified Jesus appears in white, superimposed over a black background. I place the photo on top of the map and turn it upside down, then sideways, then right side up.

"What are you looking for?" Anya asks.

"We both know that Andre believes there is information on the shroud that will lead us to the exact place where the bones are buried."

"A map," she says. "Or a diagram. Or a series of diagrams."

"Well, that's my guess. A map. But what if what we're looking for is something else entirely?"

"I'm not understanding you."

"What if the guide we're looking for is not a map or a diagram at all, but some kind of code, or series of words, or some other kind of image that's been inked into the thing?"

"What's your point?"

I take a quick glance out the window, onto the sun which is setting beyond the green, vineyard-covered hills.

"I guess my point is this: What if the answer to the location of Jesus's bones is right before me, and I can't recognize it?"

She sets her hand on top of mine.

"Don't doubt yourself so much. Let's just do the best we can, and see what we can see. If Andre couldn't find what he was looking for in a photo then chances are, neither will we. We have a unique opportunity to see the shroud up close and personal. Something my husband would have given his left nut for."

"Thank you for your confidence, Sister," I say, allowing her hand to slip into mine and squeezing it. But that's when it dawns on me. "You," I say, turning to gaze into her eyes. "You know what to look for don't you?"

She smiles.

"Maybe I do, Father," she says. "Maybe I don't. Let's just put it this way. I'll know it when I see it." Then, shifting herself so that she can point to the first, full-length photo of the shroud. "For instance, Chase, do you see this symbol written here in my husband's famous red Sharpie?"

Following the tip of her index finger she points to a nondescript triangle that's been more or less scribbled onto the photo. Only it's not a true triangle since there's no bottom to it. More like a bi-angle or, if you will, a flat, one-dimensional pyramid. Inscribed in the center of the bottomless triangle or pyramid, is a small circle. In fact, the more I stare at the photographs … the more I scan through them … the more I can see that Dr. Manion has scribbled dozens of these images on them in various or even strategic places.

"That triangle with the circle inside it," I say. "Is it a symbol?"

"You see on the shroud how many triangles and pyramid shapes exist. There are many of them. But there are also three key triangles. The first where Jesus's crucified hands meet. The second where the crucified feet meet. The third is in the place where Longinus's spear pierced him and he is said to have bled blood and water. All these areas are triangular or pyramidal in nature."

"And the circle represents the nail holes and the spear laceration." It's a question.

"Perhaps," she says. "But then look at the map of Egypt. Especially the Giza Plateau portion."

I slide the photos away and gaze down at the map. It's then something goes "click" in my brain. I can see how the geographic position of the pyramids forms a very similar triangle. In fact, the wounds on Christ line up in nearly the same position and alignment as the pyramids in the Giza Plateau. It's either a remarkable mystery how this miracle of positioning came to be or an even more remarkable coincidence. Even the Sphinx temple is laid out in the same position as the spear wound, the three tiny pyramids reserved for the wives of the Pharaohs representing the crown of thorns. Yet the pyramids were constructed thousands of years prior to Jesus's crucifixion.

Once more, I feel the fine hairs on the back of my neck rise.

So Manion was right all the time. The bones of Christ must presently be buried inside the Giza Plateau. We were closer than we thought eight years ago. But at the same time so very far away. After all, the Giza plateau is a massive place. There are literally hundreds or even thousands of chambers, tunnels, passageways, and vaults that have yet to be unearthed.

"It's quite the theory isn't it?" Anya goes on. "It's one that Andre was even banking on. But, he needed to see the Shroud for himself to know if it was true. He was convinced that not only would there be symbols giving him clues to where the bones are buried, but an actual map or blueprint made by the men and women of the 1978 Shroud inquiry, which is hopefully what we're going to find. A blueprint that would be far too small or too well concealed to show up on the average photo you can pull off of Google or Picassa."

I find myself tracing the triangular position of the pyramids and then tracing the triangular position of Christ's hands and ankles in the shroud image. Relatively speaking, they are nearly identical in position. Geometrically speaking, that is.

"Remarkable for certain," I say. "But it could all just be an amazing coincidence."

"All I can say is maybe," Anya admits. "But keep in mind that thirty-four years ago the Vatican allowed the first modern scientific examination of the shroud to occur, after centuries of stiff resistance. They even allowed samples of the shroud to be removed for the purposes of carbon dating. Don't you see? They weren't examining the shroud for authenticity. They were providing the cloth with yet the latest in the Jesus burial locations." She inches closer to me, so that her chin is nearly resting on my black leather coat-covered shoulder. "But here's where things get interesting,

Chase," she goes on. "At the very same time the shroud examination was happening in Italy, an excavation in Jerusalem was also taking place under the cover of darkness."

"Excavation," I say. "Jerusalem...You're losing me."

"Allow me to back up. In the late seventies, while foundation excavation was commencing for a new apartment complex being built in the territory between Jerusalem and Bethlehem, a tomb was unearthed. Construction immediately halted and archeologists were called in to examine its contents. Inside the tomb were uncovered nine ossuaries. All of them purportedly belonging to the family of Jesus."

The high-speed train speeds along the rails and the sky continues to grow darker, as if we were driving into the darkness and not the other way around. Anya's words are indeed incredible, but they are not altogether shocking. Anyone having anything to do with archeology ... even an old sandhog like myself ... has heard about the supposed Jesus tomb uncovered in the Holy Land many years ago. It's just that no one ever took it seriously. No one except Manion, that is. After all, he himself uncovered what he claimed was the Joseph ossuary and bones, in Egypt of all places.

"But I thought all the ossuaries were considered fabrications?" I add.

She shakes her head, vehemently.

"The find was so stunning, Chase, so insanely out of this world and, if I dare say it, so frightening, that no one knew how to handle it. Especially the member of the Israeli Antiquities Authority, the organization in charge of the dig."

"Ancestors of the very religious sect responsible for putting Jesus to death in the first place."

She nods in the affirmative. "Yes, under Caiphus whose true ossuary, incidentally, was also uncovered not far from the Jesus tomb, adding further credence to the claim."

"Holy Christ," I say, trying to keep my voice down. "The Israelis really did discover the true Jesus, didn't they? Under an apartment complex of all places."

"And the find threatened to undermine Christianity or, in other words, destroy the Jesus myth all over again. So, knowing the IAA had a potential religious time bomb on their hands they decided to simply deny the obvious. After all, nothing in archeology is one hundred percent and they knew that if they denied the truth about the mortal, physical Jesus being less than divine, than so would the rest of the world. Things would be neater and cleaner that way.

"So what did they do? The ossuaries were removed from the tomb which was then closed up, the site covered with concrete, never to be seen by human eyes again. IAA even went a step further by burying the ossuaries in a temporary unmarked grave somewhere in the hills above Jerusalem, probably near the Mount of Olives. But even an unmarked grave was considered unsafe."

"Enter the Pope," I interject.

"Exactly. By now, news of the site had hit the world vine and even though reports were suppressed as much as humanly possible, the Vatican knew they had to work closely with IAA in order to hide the evidence."

"Because you can't just destroy the bones of Jesus and his family."

"Right again, Chase. So the Vatican insisted the bones of the Jesus family be moved to a place where no one could ever possibly uncover them, unless of course they knew precisely where to look."

"And that's where the shroud comes in."

"Yes, that's where the shroud comes in. That's where it's been coming in for centuries since there has never been any one single resting place of Jesus. Even the tomb located beneath the Israeli apartment complex was not the very first and final resting place of Jesus and his immediate family."

"One question: How were the 1978 archeologists certain that the most recent Jesus tomb was that of the true Jesus family? Jesus was as common a name as Tom or John is now."

"Yes, but what made the tomb unique and certainly uncommon, is that it contained the bodies of, and I quote, Jesus son of Joseph, James brother of Jesus, Simon brother of Jesus, Joseph father of Jesus, Mary mother of Jesus and one more special person."

"Who would that be?" I ask, already knowing the answer before I hear it.

"Mary of Magdala. Jesus's wife."

I find myself reaching around and scratching the fine hairs that have for the third time in a single day, risen on the back of my neck. I feel myself shaking my head at Anya's revelation and the fact that it hasn't yet taken the world and the global religious community by storm.

"No wonder the Vatican wants to protect the bones of Jesus but at the same time, make them disappear. They've been playing this shell game for years. Eons."

"Back in 1978, the bones were dug up from the temporary grave in Jerusalem, moved under the cover of darkness across the border to Egypt and hidden in some secret vault or chamber, probably somewhere near or perhaps inside one of the ancient pyramids themselves. And judging by the Shroud wounds sharing the same position as those of the pyramids, it's more than likely that one of the pyramids was the true resting place of Jesus after he died as an old man. At least that's what Andre believes. He is convinced that when the Vatican ordered the remains back to the Giza Plateau in 1978, the Pope was essentially sending Jesus back home. Andre's beliefs were further vindicated when he uncovered the Joseph remains inside a chamber outside the Third Pyramid inside the Giza Plateau. He now believed with all his spiritual and scientific heart that although the 1978 team split the Jesus family remains up by reburying them in separate locations throughout the Plateau, the remains of Jesus were close by, nonetheless."

Yes, he did believe that. If only he had told me more. But I was his simple sandhog. I wasn't privy to the secrets. I was there to dig, along with my crew, in the spot where he told me to dig. And that was all.

"The Vatican and the IAA has been playing hide and seek the with Jesus family remains for centuries," I deduce. "Hide the bones, block any and all chances for a scientist to perform DNA testing on them. In the end, you maintain the balance of religion in both the Judeo/Christian world, and the Muslim world."

"Andre was convinced that the 1978 team working on the shroud were entrusted with marking their precise burial location on the shroud. In that sense, the shroud and the divine body it once protected in death, will have been reunited."

"What better place to record the location of the dead divinity than on its burial robe?"

In my head I'm picturing the shroud covered in maps and symbols indicating former Jesus burial locations. Or perhaps the former locations have been erased, or covered over, or they are simply too obscure or old to be noticed.

"Clever, huh?" Anya goes on. "And get this: Almost at the exact moment the bones were said to be securely reburied, the scientific examination of the shroud officially came to a close."

"Why go to such lengths to suppress the truth?"

"It's a matter of faith, Chase. No one wants to steal heaven from a man or woman dying of cancer, or from some little child's bedtime prayers. Do you?"

We sit for a bit in a silence filled with the mechanical sounds of the speeding train.

"I wonder if there's truth to the Koran? That the man who was truly crucified on Golgotha back in the first century wasn't Christ at all, but an imposter. A paid double."

"Now wouldn't that make the Vatican crumble?"

She takes hold of my hand. I feel a kind of sadness in her grip, but a tenderness also. I lean in to her, to kiss her. I would go through with it too if I don't feel a pistol barrel pressing up against my back.

13

"Don't turn around," says the man with the gun.

He's speaking the King's English mixed with a foreign accent. But the accent doesn't quite sound Italian in origin. Of course, I could be wrong about that. The Italian language consists of many dialects.

I look straight ahead, but since the sun has gone down almost entirely and the electric lighting is illuminating the car, I'm able to get a look at his reflection in the semi-tinted window glass just by glancing over my left shoulder. He's of medium height and bald. Clean shaven, as far as I can tell. Dressed entirely in dark clothing. A turtleneck and an overcoat. I have no idea what age he is. Or if it matters.

"Might I ask you your name, my son," I say.

"Cut the bullshit, Chase Baker," he giggles. "I'm well aware of who you truly are. Who the false sister is also."

"Nice to meet you, asshole," Anya says. "Maybe I should stand and start screaming about the man who has a gun pointed at my back."

"It's pointed more at Mr. Baker, actually," he corrects. "But consider a quick death aimed at you, too."

"Sixty-four-thousand-dollar question," I say. "Who are you? What do you want? Who do you work for? Are your motives political or religious or both?"

"Let's just say we all want the same thing."

"I'm just a humble servant of the Lord," I say. "You must have me mixed up for someone else."

"Those pictures of the Shroud of Turin on your lap tell a different story, my friend."

"What is it you want from us?"

"Consider me your new partner."

"I don't understand. We are people of God."

He laughs.

"You go right ahead with your charade. It will make things easier for what I am about to do."

"And what is it you are about to do?" Anya chimes in, speaking under her breath.

"I am going to accompany you to the cathedral in Turin. Once we have uncovered the secret of the shroud, you are going to show me the burial place of the true grail: The body and bones of Jesus Christ."

"When that is done?" I say.

He laughs once more.

"That will be up to God."

The train slows as we begin to enter into Milan

where we're required to switch trains. It's here we either find a way to ditch the man with the gun, or else fail at our mission.

I slowly slide my hand over to Anya. Press it against her leg.

"Take hold of your bag," I whisper.

The train slows. The travelers rise from their seats, enter into the car's narrow corridor, begin making their way towards the front of the car. The train is bucking, as though the conductor were tapping the breaks as we enter into the busy station.

Gathering up the photos and the map, I slowly shove them back inside my satchel. Then I slip the satchel strap back over my shoulder. I feel the gun poke my rib cage, only inches from my spine.

"Sit back," the man demands in a whispering scream. "Keep your hands where I can see them."

When the train comes to an abrupt, final stop, I know the time to shake the gunman is now. Fingering the seat-recline trigger located on the underside of the left-hand armrest, I quickly set my right foot up square against the seat-back in front of me and press down on my leg with all the explosiveness and power of a pole vaulter. The result is that my seat-back jams into the gunman's face.

"Go Anya!" I scream.

She doesn't hesitate. She lifts herself from the seat, her small leather bag in hand, and makes a mad dash through the queued people to the front of the car. Confused travelers fall back into the empty seats. Some shout at her. Most make way since she is dressed like nun.

I twist my body around, prop myself up on my knees, slide the 9mm from my shoulder holster, press the barrel against the man's face. His hairless face, I should say. A round face and scarred skin head that is entirely devoid of hair. The man doesn't even possess eyebrows.

People scream at the sight of the gun.

"Go!" I shout, reaching into my pocket for my passport, quick-flashing it to the panicked people. "Get off the train. I am the police and that is an order. Vai! Vai!"

The muse works. No one questions me or tries to stop me. They just get off the train as fast as they can.

I return the passport to my pocket, and at the same time, cold-cock the man across his jaw. The skin opens up on his fleshy bottom lip and the blood flows. I grab his gun, shove it into my pocket. Then I press the barrel against his forehead.

"Who are you?" I demand.

His eyes are glassy, bloodshot. These are not the eyes of a frightened or exhausted man. They are the eyes of an obsessed man. I look over my right shoulder out the window. The train platform is buzzing with alarm. I know it's only a matter of seconds before myself and this hairless man and I are made to stand down at police gunpoint.

"Are you with the Vatican?" I push, thumbing back the pistol hammer. "Tell me."

"In my left jacket pocket," he says, "you will find my identification. My country and myself have nothing to hide."

I dig for it, pull out the wallet, flick it open.

There's a laminated ID in the place where a photograph of a loved one might go. The man's photograph is included in the ID, along with his name: Lee Einhorn, Senior Archaeologist, Israeli Antiquities Authority.

One more look out the window. Two policemen have arrived. They are drawing their weapons while directing the onlookers to move away.

"What you're doing is not only illegal," Einhorn spits, "it is very dangerous. You have no idea the firestorm you will unleash upon the world should you uncover the bones of Christ. You will upset a delicate balance that has existed for thousands of years. Legions of people have already died believing in Christ as divine. Now, if you make him human, even more will die defending his humanity or lamenting what will be only a future of blackness. Don't you see? I must stop you as others surely will attempt."

Another glance at the glass. I know the cops are about to board the train.

"Not if I can help it, Einhorn," I say, tossing his ID back at him. "The world is going to blow itself to hell no matter what I dig up. Always been that way and always will be." I can't help but feel myself smiling. "'Sides, there's a lot of money at stake."

I hear the sound of footsteps bounding the three metal steps up into the car.

I pocket my weapon. Sliding out of the seat, I turn and head straight for the exit as the policemen make the ninety-degree turn into the car's interior.

"In there, Officer," I say, pulling down on the

satchel strap. "Thank God almighty you are here."

The police brush past me and burst into the car. I take the stairs down to the platform, my eyes seeking out Anya. She's standing behind the crowd of onlookers at the area where the platform connects with the main station.

I make my way towards her, never looking back.

Not even once.

14

"You okay?" I ask, as I take hold of her arm.

"I'm a nun," she says. "Suffering is my life."

I take a look up at the giant electronic Departures/Arrivals billboard mounted to the station's polished stone interior. The Turin train has arrived at Platform 2 and is now boarding.

"Shit," I say. "Damn train is scheduled to depart at 7:05pm." I shoot a glance at my wristwatch. "That's one minute ago."

"We'll have to wait for the next one," Anya says.

"Let's go," I say, taking hold of her hand.

"The platform is all the way on the other side of the station, Chase. We'll never make it."

"Run, sister, run!"

We make our way through the throngs of travelers and commuters going in and out of Milan station. Mixed in with the people are the many polizia who have arrived to investigate the man who pulled a gun on some unsuspecting Roman Catholic clergy on the incoming arrival from Florence. We move on in the direction of the number 2 platform, our shoulders slamming into the shoulders and arms of the people who move too slow, or who come at us in the opposite direction. I know that under normal circumstances people would be yelling at us, swearing, shoving us back, if not for our divine costumes.

I spot the platform.

"The train is leaving," Anya huffs.

"We'll make it," I insist, pulling her arm even harder.

We round the corner onto the platform as the train strains to begin its forward movement out of the station.

"Come on!" I shout. "Come! On!"

The doors on the first car have yet to be closed all the way. Reaching out, I manage to get a handhold on it while jumping up onto the landing platform.

"I can't make it!" Anya screams, her hand still gripped in mine as she runs, keeping pace with train. "You go. I will meet you!"

"No," I insist. "Someone will get to you. The police or the gunman."

I yank on her arm as the train picks up speed. I feel her losing her balance, her footing. I feel myself losing her entirely. Only one choice: Bracing myself I yank her up and onto the platform, the both of us collapsing onto the metal steps. I take my foot away and the door closes. The both of us lie there, looking at one another. We look into one another's eyes. I kiss her then. Rather, she kisses me, our tongues moving in and out of one another's mouth, our beating hearts pressed together. When we come up for air, we smile. It's a crazy scene. Absurd even. A nun and a priest kissing one another on the steps of a speeding train car.

"We'd better get up before we get caught," Anya says.

"Amen to that," I say, watching her lift herself up and gather her black bag.

I stand, straighten out my satchel on my shoulder, and together we go in search of our seating assignments. In one half-hour's time, we will arrive in Turin. With the help of God or fate, the shroud key will be revealed.

15

We arrive in Turin on schedule.

It's dark out now. Foggy. The fog laps the curved cobbled roads like a gray/black tongue while the inverted arcs of sodium lamp light spewing forth from the black, metal street fixtures create an eerie misty glow. As we make our way on foot away from the train station towards the cathedral, I can't help but feel the dark silence that seems to drape this place like the shroud it houses. To say it feels different here is an understatement of Biblical proportions. Pun intended. This is a holy place if ever there was one. It radiates with an electric spirit, the memory of a soul that shook the world two thousand years ago and continues to shake it today.

Already we can make out the towering spires of the Cathedral. As we approach it, I keep wide eyes out for a secure hiding place for my 9mm and the revolver I stripped from the IAA gunman on the train. I locate one in the form of a dumpster. A blue, heavy-duty plastic box set beside a second identical box. One for paper, the other for glass and metals. Reaching into my black leather coat, I unclasp the shoulder holster, pull it off. Bending at the knees, I set the holster and the gun it carries onto the dumpster's undercarriage. Then I set the revolver beside it. Standing, I button my coat.

"The truth about Jesus," I say to myself more than Anya. "It resides inside that old church."

We stand before the great stone cathedral. But, instead of climbing the stairs to its heavy wood doors, we make our way around a perimeter surrounded by an iron fence until we come to a guard shack and the two armed guards who protect it.

"This is it," I whisper under my breath. "Don't say anything you don't need to say."

"You're the expert, Ren Man," Anya whispers. "It's what I'm paying you for."

"Good evening," I say, standing before the first guard. He's taller than me, slimmer, younger. Meaner looking too.

"Buono sera," he utters, but I'm not so sure he means it.

I smile, even if it's the last thing I feel like doing on earth.

"Please," I say. "Our Italian is not so good. I am Father John Crews and this is my associate Sister Rosaire de Maria. We are here to see the shroud."

The guard turns to gaze over his shoulder at the shorter, but meatier second guard.

Then, turning back to me.

"Do you have an appointment at this late hour? No one sees the shroud without a special appointment."

"But, of course," I say, reaching into the interior pocket of my leather coat, producing the forged documentation. "Natalia is expecting us."

The guard gazes down at the documentation. In Italian, he asks the second guard if he knows anything about our arrival. The second guard shakes his head.

"Wait here," orders the first guard.

We do as he says.

He steps into the guard shack, picks up a phone receiver, presses it to his ear. He speaks something into the phone all the while keeping a careful eye on us through the glass wall, as if the burly second guard watching over us with his automatic weapon isn't enough.

After a few weighted seconds, the first guard hangs the phone up, steps out of the shack.

"Let them pass," he directs the second guard.

The electronic operated gate opens, and as Anya and I step on through, a woman emerges from out of the dark mist. She's coming towards us at a light jog.

"Father Crews!" she bellows. "Sister Rosaire de Maria! How wonderful that you have made it here safely."

She's the tall blonde that Checco described for me. The same woman I recognize by the many multi-media text photos he's sent my way detailing their recent love affair. She's taller than the both of us and voluptuously built, like so many Russian women. Especially Moscovites. While eyeing the guards, she takes Anya by the hand like they are intimate friends.

"That will be all for now gentlemen," she says, in her Russian-accented English. Then, leading us up towards the rectory. "Come, come … You must be hungry and tired. Let's rest a bit and eat something before you see the shroud."

We walk until out of earshot of the guards. That's when Natalia changes her tone.

"I'm not sure what your mission here is," she says, her mood suddenly unfeeling and direct, "and why it's so important that you must come here tonight and upset everything. But I owe Checco a special favor. This will be the favor."

We face a solid metal door that's operated by a key-code and a retinal scanner. Looking up, I can see just one of what, no doubt, are many wall-mounted security cameras that are eyeing both Anya and I in real-time. I try not to look directly into it.

Natalia positions her right eye before the retinal scanner so that it's able to pick up her ID in a quick flash of ultraviolet light. Stepping back, the door unbolts. The Russian woman pushes it open, steps inside.

"Follow me," she insists.

Unlike the exterior of this Cathedral which is hundreds of years old, she leads us down a corridor that is constructed of concrete, steel, and glass. Illuminating it are ceiling-mounted sodium lamps. The walls, ceilings and floor are painted white so that it gives off the feel of heaven. That is, if heaven turns out to be part house of God, part reinforced concrete bunker. I had always been under the impression that a team of Franciscan monks had been assigned by the Vatican to watch over the shroud. Thus far anyway, I have yet to see a single monk.

Natalia leads us down the length of the corridor to a hallway that's situated perpendicular to it. We hook a right and follow her for a few feet more until we come to another solid metal door. This one belonging to an office.

Like Natalia was required to do for entry into the sacristy, she punches in a key-code on the wall-mounted device and once more scans her right eye. When the door unlocks she holds it open for us, asks us to enter into the room before her.

We do it.

If the corridor looks and feels like an underground bunker, this room definitely serves as the war room. A high-tech room you might find in the basement of the White House. The walls are black, the lighting canned and dim. The far wall supports a row of large LCD monitors that not only portray every possible angle of the shroud, but every conceivable pathway to it. The monitors not focused on the shroud, are focused instead on the cathedral's exterior. There's even a satellite image of the rooftop. A uniformed guard sits in a leather-backed swivel chair. He's obviously in charge of controlling the monitors.

"This is our operations center," Natalia begins to explain. "As you can plainly see, there is no possible way for anyone to get near the shroud without being spotted. The cathedral is armed with only the tightest security, and despite our holy mission, they do maintain an order of shoot-to-kill and ask questions later. Am I understood?"

"Thought you said we were going to eat something?" I say.

She cracks a hint of a smile.

"Do not test my patience, Mr. Baker," Natalia warns. "I owe Checco a favor for a very good reason. I am providing it for him." Now looking at her watch. "However, that favor runs out in precisely fifteen minutes. Do we understand one another?"

I glance down at my watch. It's 7:45 PM.

"I guess at eight o'clock we all become pumpkins," I say.

"We'll try our hardest to be quick," Anya interjects.

Natalia nods.

"One moment," she says.

Turning, she goes to the uniformed security guard who is manning the monitor controls. She whispers something into his ear. When she's through, he stands, pushes back his chair, and without offering us so much as a sideways glance, leaves the room. That's when Natalia sits down at the controls, places both her hands on the keyboard. Typing in a series of commands, the LCD monitors go dead.

She stands.

"Let's move," she demands. "Fifteen minutes and counting."

We follow her out of the room, back into the corridor. She turns to the left and quickly begins making her way to the corridor's opposite end. We come upon yet another steel door with a light embedded in the upper center. The door is protected with more security cameras and entry devices. Natalia punches in her code and scans her right eye yet again. The door opens onto a cool, dark, and musty room.

It's the sacristy to the Chapel of the Shroud.

"Behold the most cherished relic of the holy Roman Catholic Church," she says. Then, with one more glance at her watch. "Thirteen minutes."

The second most cherished relic, I wanted to say. *That is, the mortal remains of Jesus actually exist.*

I step inside, Anya on my heels. The door slams shut behind me. I look directly ahead at the vague, one-dimensional image of a man positioned horizontally on his right side and quickly come to realize this isn't a man at all.

This is God.

16

"Time is not luxury at present," Anya says, approaching the illuminated rectangular, gold-rimmed glass box that houses the 4.4 meter by 1.1 meter linen cloth bearing the blood-soaked image of the crucified Jesus. She has the smartphone Checco provided for her in hand, and she immediately begins using its camera app to snap away at the body, starting with the feet on the left-hand side and making her way along the length of the body.

I, on the other hand, look for something else. Look for it with the naked eye.

Inscriptions. Drawings. Symbols. Maps...

"I need something to stand on," I say, looking over both shoulders.

I spot some black chairs pressed up against the sacristy wall. I grab hold of one of the chairs, position it in front of the faint image. With the naked eye I scan several medallion symbols and some calligraphy. All of which were included in Manion's collection of photographs. But nothing that would lead me to believe it describes the location of the remains.

"How we doing on time?" Anya begs, while snapping away, knowing that if we don't find what we've come for she might at the very least uncover something with her camera.

I glance at my watch once more.

"Seven minutes," I say, my eyes never leaving the image.

I focus my search on the triangular shapes and patterns that Manion was so suspicious of. I examine the center of Christ's body, the triangle formed by his wrists. I examine the triangle that's formed by his right arm, the fingers on his left hand, and his spear-pierced side. Then I examine the triangle formed by his crucified ankles, his long legs and his waist.

I take a step back and look at the cloth as a whole and try and picture the layout of the Giza Pyramids, how their topographical layout matches that of the Christ wounds almost precisely. But, even if they do match, I'm still not getting anything that suggests a specific resting place of the bones within the confines of the Giza Plateau.

"I'm not seeing anything in the triangles," I say.

"Ignore them," Anya says. "Focus outside the triangles."

I search the perimeter of the long cloth. I run up one side and down the other, gazing at areas damaged in not just one fire over the centuries but if my history serves me right, two fires, both of which nearly threatened to destroy the sacred relic. I decide to once more start at the feet and work my way sideways. That's when I catch it at the very bottom of the shroud. A series of angular lines and circles that haven't been sewn into the linen cloths, but that appear to have been tattooed right beside Jesus's left foot. The faint blue lines and circles can't possibly take up more than the width of a couple of thumbprints, and there's no way in God's holy heaven you would notice them if you weren't looking for a map of some kind. But if you had grown up in the excavating and sandhogging business like I did and you knew what a blueprint looked like, you would know that you just struck paydirt.

"I've got it, Anya."

She comes to me.

"Lean down," I say, pointing to the blue lines and circles. "You see it?"

"I'm straining my eyes," she says.

"Just take a picture of where my finger is positioned," I say. "Do it now. We only have two minutes left."

She does it.

"Now let me see your phone," I add.

She hands it to me.

I stare down at the digital photograph. I enhance and enlarge it by pressing my finger-pads against the screen and moving them outwards. The photograph enlarges. These are most definitely the lines of a miniature computer-generated blueprint. An early generation CAD rendering, most likely originating from the late 1970s. That's when it begins to make sense. I see what could very well be the base of a pyramid and several chambers that extend underground. Inside the bottom-most room is contained a symbol. *The* symbol. It's a bottomless triangle with a circle in the center. The location of Jesus's body. Or so I can only assume.

"Time," Anya says. "Ten seconds at most."

"We've got what we came for," I say, grabbing her hand. "Let's move."

We go to the door. I grip the closer, try and turn it.

That's when the peace and sanctity of the chapel sacristy explodes in automatic gunfire.

17

There's comes a scream that's followed by a dreadful silence.

A dead silence.

When I peer out the door's safety glass, I see a man lying on the corridor floor in a pool of his own blood. It's the uniformed guard who until moments ago, had been operating the monitors. I see another man come around the corner, walking at a stride and gait that seems as if he owns the joint. It's the hairless man from the train. Einhorn, the IAA man. He must have gotten away from the police and followed us here on the same train. How he managed to dodge the Milan police and make the train, I have no idea. I only know that he is here. Here now. He's got an automatic gripped in both hands, combat position, and he's approaching the door with it.

I take a step back as he raises the weapon up, triggers off a burst of rounds which embed themselves into the metal door.

"Stay down!" I shout at Anya.

She pulls off her veil, tosses it to the sacristy floor.

"We need guns," she says.

"We're S.O.L." I say. "Until we get out of here, grab the ones I hid under the dumpster."

Another burst of gunfire. Another series of rounds bury themselves into the steel door, cracking the safety-glass light. Then comes another shot. A single shot that sounds far different from the automatic. I make out the deadweight slump sound of a body as it drops to the concrete floor.

The door opens.

It's Natalia. She's a big, beautiful blonde apparition gripping an AR15 like she knows how to use it. And she does. There's a swirl of white smoke rising up from out of the barrel.

"Come with me," she orders.

She goes past the shroud, to a thick, ornately carved, dark wood door. Unlocking the door, she waves us on through. We enter into the main chapel and become immediately surrounded in a gaseous cloud of smoldering incense. We're standing on the back altar, but there's a protective glass screen or shield that will prevent us from simply making our way out of the old cathedral through the front wood doors. I can only assume the glass shield is bullet proof. Probably grenade proof considering the relic it guards.

"You aren't seeing this," Natalia says,

approaching the ornate, two-story, gold-gilded high altar piece. Placing her security card into an almost invisible slot on the alter-piece, a secret door of approximately five feet by three feet slowly opens. It's the kind of thing you only see in Hollywood.

"What is this?" I say.

"It's a secret tunnel for transporting the shroud should the church be attacked by pirates looking to steal it or by fanatics who wish to destroy it for the secrets it bears. The Vatican maintains a tunnel just like it for the Pope. A tunnel that leads from the depths of Saint Peter's Basilica all the way to Hadrian's castle. The tunnel was utilized constantly all the way up through World War Two."

"My guess is the Vatican possesses more than one secret tunnel."

"It's also a safeguard against something like a fire breaking out which it did in this very sacristy in 1978 by an unnamable arsonist. If this tunnel wasn't here at that time, the shroud would have been lost forever."

"1978," Anya states. "That year seems to resonate an awful lot as of late."

"I'm thinking the soldiers of the Vatican," I add. "Soldiers who might not represent the Pope and his wishes, but who nonetheless are willing to go to extreme lengths to keep the divine mystery of Jesus a true mystery. They might fit the bill as the arsonists. They and/or the IAA."

"These stairs will lead you to a tunnel," she says. "Follow it until you come to a second set of stairs. Climb the stairs. You will know what to do when you get to the top."

"You first Anya," I say.

"Nice time for you to start being a gentleman, Ren Man," she quips.

The door is small, so that she is forced to enter into it at a crouch. I enter behind her. So close I am touching her backside.

"You're not coming?" I say, turning to Natalia.

"My job is to protect the shroud at all costs," she explains. "I also have a body to dispose of. These are not matters for the police, as you can imagine."

I reach out my hand.

"Thank you," I say.

She takes the hand, squeezes it gently but firmly.

"I hope you found what you were after. The shroud has many secrets and many answers. It can be a dangerous object in the wrong hands, but a source of illumination in the right hands. It rarely reveals anything to anyone, other than to those who are the most devout."

"I haven't said a prayer in thirty years," I confess.

"Prayers don't always have to be spoken to be heard and answered."

I release my hand.

She goes to close the small door.

"Natalia," I say. "One more thing."

The door opens again.

"Quickly," she says.

"The favor you owed Checco," I say. "It must have been one hell of a favor to do what you did for us. To place yourself and the shroud in such danger. Do you mind my asking why you owe him so much?"

She grins, almost sadly.

"I'm carrying his child," she reveals.

She closes the door, locks it. For a brief moment we are bathed in a darkness so thick, I cannot make out Anya who crouches only inches from me. Then a light comes on. Correction ... A series of caged light fixtures that are mounted to the concrete wall and that seem to run the length of the tunnel.

"Next stop, Cairo," I say to Anya.

She begins the climb down the narrow staircase. I can't help but think about Natalia's words. About praying without knowing it. About believing in something for which I have no proof. About having faith, even if I question my belief in God.

My heart in my throat and apparently, my soul beside it, I make the climb down the concrete stairs.

18

Once down the stairs, it's a straight shot through a narrow, low-ceilinged tunnel. The dimly lit tunnel runs for maybe a half mile before it ends at another staircase, this one shaped like a corkscrew that wraps around a concrete pilaster. When we reach the top, we face yet another steel door. The door is not only closed, it bears no opener.

Anya turns to me, her smooth, tan face beginning to show the first signs of physical stress. Judging by the newly formed creases around her almond-shaped eyes.

"What now?" she inquires.

"Try knocking," I suggest.

"Knock," she says. "That's your solution? Just knock like we're asking the next door neighbor if we can borrow some sugar?"

"Got a better idea, sweetness?"

Raising up her right arm, she makes a fist with her hand and raps on the door with her knuckles. Three solid knocks. She's right. It's as if she were paying a visit to her next door neighbor. The bone against hollow metal echoes in the vertical stairwell.

We wait for a long few seconds. Until we hear the sound of deadbolts being released.

Anya steps back, so that her back is pressed against me. It's not a bad feeling having her so close to me. So close I can feel my heart beating against her body.

The door opens.

The bearded, late-middle-aged man standing inside the open door is short and somewhat round. He's wearing loose dungarees, work boots and a work shirt with an apron draped over it, like a butcher might wear. But this apron is not stained with blood.

"Come with me," he demands.

Without a word we follow him up yet another, shorter set of stairs until we come to a set of Bilco basement doors that have already been opened. The man climbs through first with us on his tail. When we come to the top, I can see that we're not inside a butcher shop, but a working newsstand that's part of a larger three-roomed shack.

The man quickly closes the egress doors and padlocks them. He then covers them with a thick rug.

"Help me with something," he orders in broken English while taking his place on the opposite end of a large wooden harvest table.

I grab hold of the opposite side of the table and

together we lift it and set in onto the rug. The table has some food on it. Some meats and cheeses, along with a bottle of red wine.

He tells us to eat something.

"What's your name?" I ask.

"Call me, Carlo," he says. "I will be escorting you to the airport. Your flight leaves for Cairo in two hours."

In my head, I'm recalling the guns I left behind under the dumpster. I tell Carlo about them.

"Don't worry," he says. "We will pick them up and hold onto them for you."

"What do I do for weaponry in Cairo?"

"You will be greeted by a man right outside your gate. His name is Sameh. He will be your fixer and your confidant. He will take care of everything. Do you understand?"

I nod.

"Thank you."

He smiles.

"Don't thank me. I am getting paid for my services as are you. Thank your friend, Checco."

Anya turns to me.

"Checco's quite the character," she comments. "He certainly knows how to spend my dead dad's money, doesn't he?"

"Wait until you get his bill," I say, turning to her. Then, turning back to Carlo. "Is there somewhere we can change out of these holy clothes?"

In my mind I'm picturing the lug-soled boots, dark Levis work shirt, and leather bomber I lugged with me in my satchel. No doubt Anya is dying to ditch the nun's habit.

He nods to a room off the back.

"You first," I say to Anya.

In the meantime, I pour a glass of wine, and eat some cheese. The first food I've consumed in many hours. Carlo excuses himself while he tends to some customers demanding train tickets out in front of the newsstand. I sip the wine and try to make sense of this whole thing. As far as we know, Manion is somewhere Egypt. In the desert outside of Cairo, digging in a location on behalf a wealthy Muslim Brotherhood kidnapper that is almost certainly a wrong location. My guess is that Manion knows he's digging in the wrong place and that he's simply stalling the inevitable: The moment when his kidnappers get so frustrated with him, they put a bullet in his head.

But I've been commandeered by the Florence Polizia to locate Manion before that happens. Nowhere in my present job description does it call for my locating the Holy Grail—the true bones of Jesus. But the problem is this: It's in my blood to go after the bones. I am digger by trade, but I am hunter also. Denying my chance at the bones is like asking me not to breathe. Without even realizing it at the time, I had a chance to go after the bones once before, and blew it. Now a second chance has fallen into my lap.

But then, I'm not a cold-hearted greedy son of a bitch either.

My religiously devout parents raised me better than that. I've promised to locate Manion and I will do so. But once that mission is accomplished, I'm going after the bones. If Manion and his ex-wife wish to accompany me, all the better. I might be able to deduce the location of the bones via the blueprint I pulled off the shroud. But I have no idea what to expect once we get to the site. No idea what to look out for, be it booby traps, natural obstacles, or certain death itself. One thing is for sure, no matter where they lay, the bones won't simply be there for the taking. We will have to work for them. Work for them harder than we've ever worked in our lives. That will take strength, but it will also take courage and brains. That's why I need Manion, and that's why I need him alive.

Anya emerges from out of the back room. She's back to her black jeans, lace-up boots, and leather jacket over a simple black T-shirt. She is as beautiful as the night is long. She takes my hand.

"Better get dressed, Ren Man," she says. "We'll be leaving soon."

I lean in, kiss her on the mouth. She tastes sweet, her lips as soft as my melting heart.

"You're falling in love," I say.

"Bite your tongue. I'm not that easy. But then, unlike you, I'm not that hard either."

I hold back a laugh on my way to the back room.

19

We're transported by car under the cover of darkness to the Turin International Airport and soon we are airborne for the four hour trip to Cairo. We land just as dawn is arriving on the new day and the sun is rising bright orange over the desert, melting the coolness that no doubt settled in over the night and replacing it with a heavy, laden heat.

As promised we are greeted outside the baggage claim doors by a young man named Sameh. The tall, muscular, black-haired man doesn't greet us with secrecy like one might expect. Instead he holds up a white cardboard sign with the name CHASE written on it in thick black Sharpie.

So much for keeping our heads safely under the local radar...

After sharing some quick greetings, Anya and I follow our contact out of the airport and into the

121

heat of the early morning. Seating us in the back of his white sedan, we head out into Cairo's notoriously heavy traffic. To say the traffic is thick here is like saying the Sinai desert contains some sand. Traffic is everywhere and it is non-stop. It seems to take on a life of its own, like a mechanical river of moving metal parts, choking smoke, and noise. It's so chaotic, dense, and even dangerous, that Sameh uses his horn not to draw attention of someone he wants out of the way or someone who is about to run into him, but for communicating specific messages. One beep for "How's it going?" Two long beeps for "Wake up, you're about to smash into me." One long extended beep for "Move or by the grace of Allah, I will run you down!" This isn't my first trip to Cairo. My first trip goes back all the way to the mid-1970s when I was just a boy and my father was sandhogging for some university archaeologists who were working on the Theban Mapping Project in the Valley of the Kings. So I've learned the road ropes by now.

As we crawl along, Sameh peers at us through the mirror.

"I have secured a hotel for you. The Kings Hotel. Very close to Giza."

I know the place since I've stayed there a half dozen times before. An old time hotel better suited for journalists, adventurers, and private antiquities collectors who deal only in cash and who prefer to keep to themselves. No questions asked. It also houses one of the only remaining bars in an ever increasingly militantly Muslim Cairo.

"Private antiquities collectors?" Anya poses.

"Treasure hunters," I say. Then, "What about a weapon, Sameh?"

"I have all of that covered, naturally. Plus a laptop computer....Checco filled me in on everything required of my services."

Anya leans into me, whispers into my ear. "Every time I hear that name, I picture piles of one-hundred dollar bills going up in smoke."

"But it's money well burnt," I whisper back.

I think about the photos we've taken of the shroud. How important it will be to match the small blueprint up with a detailed plan of one of the three Giza pyramid interiors, should I be able to locate just such an interior plan. And it's possible I know just the place to find one.

"Why aren't we headed to Giza right now?" Anya asks, setting her hand on mine.

"It's important that I see a man first," I insist. "A man whom I've worked with on occasion when digging in and around Cairo for various clients. A man named Amun. If anyone knows about a dig being sponsored by the Muslim Brotherhood using a kidnaped American as the lead archeologist, it will be Amun. He might be one of the sleaziest men I know, but he will prove instrumental in our finding your husband. There's a lot of desert out there. Anything else is just entering into a wild goose chase."

But what I also know is that he will help me with finding the exact location of the bones should the blueprint pulled from the shroud turn out to be authentic.

Anya removes her hand.

"I'm just anxious is all," she says. "I'll be able to breathe better once we find Andre."

She looks out the window onto the stream of cars and trucks, their beds filled with people, crates of chickens and other live—and not so live—cargo. In between the vehicles, boys and men scoot around on motorbikes. Some people take a chance on running in between the moving cars, Chinese made pickups, and Jeeps.

It takes almost an hour to drive the relatively short distance from the airport to Tahrir Square. Throughout history, this spot has been the ground-zero for demonstrations, revolutions and riots. Today is no exception. From my perch in Sameh's shotgun seat, it looks like a war zone. There's a throng of Arab protestors gathered around several consulates, including what I know to be the American facility. The men cover their faces with black cloth and they wear scarves over their heads. They look like bandits. Some are tossing rocks at the U.S. embassy gates and over brick walls which are covered in razor-sharp concertina wire. Some of the masked men grip AK47s, which they point towards the Arab sky, fingering live rounds into the air. In the near distance, a tall office building is blackened and still smoking from a fire. People are shouting and screaming.

"Keep your heads down back there," Sameh warns. "This has been going on for days. People are dying in the streets."

Tahrir Square isn't really a true square at all, but a large oval with a roundabout in its center. I've spent some time here in the past, so I'm well aware that all manner and types of buildings from many different eras make up the perimeter of the square, including a dozen or more consulates and embassies. The Egyptian Museum is located on the square, and so is the Arab League Headquarters, plus the House of Folklore, and even the American University which was thriving the last time I was here, but that now is an empty shell of its former academic glory.

"What are they protesting right now?" Anya begs.

"The same thing they've been protesting for more than a year," Sameh says, his hands tightly gripping the wheel. "The president has taken it upon himself to rewrite the constitution while assuming supreme power. While some celebrate the return of true, militant Islamic rule to the country, others see the President's declaration of supreme power as the first act in an inevitable civil war between militant Islamists and supporters of a free democratic republic. Our economy is in a shambles. There's no food, or gas, or jobs. You could almost say the Muslim Brotherhood is propping up a modern day pharaoh while tearing down the country."

"The Muslim Brotherhood," I say to her. "These are the same people who have taken away your ex-husband."

A barrage of automatic gunfire startles us. It comes from directly behind us. Turning in my seat, I see a gang of black-bearded and scarved men. They're making fists with one hand, and waving AKs with the other. They're coming up on our car.

"For the love of Allah," Sameh laments. He

presses his foot on the gas, but there's nowhere to go. Not if he doesn't want to smash into the car ahead of him. He lays on the horn. One long, solid honk.

Get the hell out of the way...

The angry gang is getting closer.

"What do they have against us?" begs Anya.

"They know my car," Sameh says. "They know it is the car of a fixer... A guide."

"Let me guess. A guide for westerners and infidels," Anya adds, her face peering out the back window.

The gang is on us now. They're pounding on the hood with the butts of the AKs. Screaming and shouting in obscenities I cannot begin to make out, but I somehow understand nonetheless.

Sameh is visibly sweating, the beads forming on his forehead and streaking down his dark face. I don't like seeing my fixer like this. It means we're in real danger.

I put my hand on the door. Maybe it's time we make a run for it.

"No Chase!" he screams. "Don't do it. They will maul you, drag you away and beat you ... They will beat and rape Anya. They will take me away and kill me."

I feel my heart lodging itself in my throat.

Anya has grown pale.

"You have a gun?" I ask.

"No," he says. "Not here."

"Then just do something."

To our right is the gravel and sand-covered center of the round-about. Back when I was a kid, the center supported a giant fountain that rivaled something you might find in downtown Rome. But in more recent times, the fountain has been ripped out and replaced with a giant statue of the much revered Muslim leader, Omar Makram. Makram is famous for having kicked the crap out of Napoleon's troops in a battle waged amidst the pyramids of the Giza Plateau. Behind Omar, are planted some flag poles which used to support the flags of the free world. Only there are no longer any flags flying in the wind, since it's quite obvious the symbols of the free world have been pulled down, spit on, and burned.

Sameh turns the wheel to the right, hits the gas, drives up onto the gravelly center and guns it. The mob who occupies it is forced to move to the side in one giant wave, or else risk being mowed down and martyred unintentionally. But one man separates himself from the mob, holds his ground, aims the black barrel of his automatic rifle at us.

"Down!" Sameh screams. "Get! Down!"

I grab the collar on Anya's leather jacket, pull her down onto me. I don't hear the two rounds that burst through the front and rear windshields above our heads, so much as I feel them fly past.

"You still with us, Sameh?" I bark.

"Thank Allah," he says, turning the wheel one way and then another, the car fishtailing over the grass and gravel, but somehow moving forward. I feel a heavy thump, and I know the car has dropped back down onto road.

I sit up, enough to peer through the windshield. "Where the hell are we?"

"1973 Victory Bridge," he informs. "We've made it out of the square with our lives. You can breathe now."

Brushing shards of glass off her shoulders, Anya sits up.

"You okay?" I ask.

"Welcome to Cairo," she says. "I thought this place was supposed to be a tourist's paradise on earth."

I can see she's trying to look on the bright side, but failing miserably.

"Most of the tourists are long gone," I say, feeling the beads of sweat pouring down my face, tasting the salt on my lips. "Back when I was a kid I could walk the streets of Cairo alone and not worry about a thing."

"Back when I was a kid," Anya says, "I was lucky if my parents took an out of town vacation at all."

Sameh cuts a quick left and proceeds down a narrow alley. We pass a butcher shop to my right, three skinned goat carcasses hanging from its exterior rafters. The butcher is squatting on the gravelly ground, smoking shisha from a tin-bellied hookah. To my left, a small group of three black burka-clad women move to the side for us. They don't look at us for fear of making eye contact with the driver. The driver is a man after all, and only their husbands are allowed to look into their eyes.

We speed down a half dozen more alleys, taking too many rights and hooking way too many lefts to make sense of, until we come to a full stop outside the short flight of stairs that access a humble concrete high-rise consisting of maybe nine or ten stories. The neon sign mounted to building's exterior reads "Kings Hotel." There's an armed guard standing at the top of the stairs. He's dressed in police whites topped off with a black beret.

Sameh gets out, opens the door for Anya.

I exit the vehicle, and take a quick look around. Located directly across the street from the hotel is an old mansion built during the Victorian French occupation. It's surrounded by brick and iron walls. Several machine gun-armed guards watch over it. There are cars parked in the streets, some of them bombed or burned out and left to rot. Others have become resting places for the many wild dogs that roam the streets looking for an easy meal, or an unlucky rodent to cross the road.

We have no bags other than what we're carrying, so Anya and I proceed up the stairs behind Sameh. When we enter into the lobby, we feel the coolness of the ceiling fans circulating the air around the dim, stone-tiled room. To our right, the long bar is crowded with khaki and bush-jacketed men, drinking the morning away.

"Here are the keys to your room," he says, handing us one metal key apiece. "I assume you would like to freshen up. I will wait for you in the bar."

"Thanks for taking care of us back there," I tell him. "Have one on me."

He smiles, his dark eyes rich and genuine.

"That's my job," he offers. "You will have a whiskey waiting for you when you return."

"Make that two whiskeys, Sameh," Anya adds.

My employer and I make for the elevators, knowing our work in a very unsafe Egypt has only just begun.

20

The room is small, but spacious enough for two people who barely know one another. There is only one queen-sized bed, so that will have to do, should we even get the chance to use it. Set on the desk is a laptop computer and a large manila envelope which has been sealed with clear packing tape. While Anya uses the bathroom to freshen up, I go to the package, tear the top open. Inside I find a 9mm Smith and Wesson automatic. My preferred brand of hand cannon precisely. Plus two extra ammo mags of nine rounds apiece. There's also a USB cord and a stack of Egyptian pounds. Slipping the pistol into my pant waist, I stuff the ammo mags into the right pocket of my leather bomber, and the cash into my left trouser pocket. I also use the opportunity to change out the SIM card on my Droid. Anya's phone is made by Samsung which means changing her card is out of the question. Such are the risks inherent in our quest.

When Anya emerges from the bath, she doesn't look happy.

"There was barely a trickle of water," she points out.

"Get used to it. You're not gonna find Carnival Cruises traveling up and down the Nile anytime soon. You saw what was happening in Tahrir Square. We barely made it out of there alive. Cairo and much of Egypt is a post-revolution wreck."

I ask her for her smartphone. She pulls it out of her bag and hands it to me. I then proceed to download the shroud photos. When it's done a few seconds later, I hand her back the phone. I had avoided pulling the Giza map out on the plane or, for that matter, going over the photos we took of the shroud. I had no idea who might be following us. Who might be watching. Now we're surrounded by four walls. Now will be as safe as things get, until we once more board a plane out of Cairo.

I bring up the photo of the blueprint located on the bottom right-hand of the shroud. Now that it's downloaded to a computer I'm able to blow it up and get a perfect look at it.

"What's that look like to you?" I pose to Anya.

She leans in, stares at the screen.

"Like a series of chambers leading down into the depths of the earth."

I Google the Giza pyramids and search for a site that contains illustrations of the documented interior chambers of all three. I am immediately able to eliminate both the Great Pyramid and the Second slightly smaller pyramid since their interior chambers and tunnels are far different from what's displayed on the shroud CAD diagram. But the third, and the smallest of the three pyramids, is different.

"That's it," Anya says. "The third pyramid. The pyramid of Menkaure."

"Different but the same," I say.

"I don't understand."

"The layout on the shroud is the exact opposite of the Third pyramid."

That's when I find myself reaching into my right trouser pocket. Pulling out the ancient half-mirror I acquired in the Giza Plateau eight years ago, I hold it up to the computer screen.

"Look at it now."

Anya grabs hold of my shoulder, squeezes.

"It's identical."

"The scholars printed the blueprint in reverse."

"Why would they do that?"

"We're talking the bones of Jesus, here. If the bones are located inside that chamber, we're going to have to work for them. Diversions and false leads will haunt us the entire way. Which is why it's so important we find your husband and find him soon."

Anya grabs hold of my arm.

"It's important we find him because he's a human being whose life is in danger," she scolds. "I'm beginning to think that you set your sights on a bag of bones from the very beginning and haven't taken them off since."

I gaze down at her hand hold. Slowly, she

removes it.

"You're right," I say. "You're husband's safety before all else."

"Thank you, Chase," she says, pursing her lips. "But if only I believed you."

Typing in a series of commands on the laptop, I make a printout of the shroud blueprint, stuff it into the breast pocket of my shirt. The pocket over my heart. Standing, I pull the pistol out of my belt, thumb the clip release, check the load. Slapping the clip back into its housing, I pull back on the action, load a round into the chamber and engage the safety.

Anya looks at me with a frown and squinted eyes.

"What's wrong?" I say, placing the gun back into my pant waist.

"I don't like guns," she says.

"You like your life?"

"Sure."

"Then learn to like guns. One of them may save your life one day. Or help save the life of your ex-husband."

Grabbing my satchel I toss the strap over my shoulder and head for the door.

21

As promised, Sameh is waiting for us at the bar. Two whiskeys also await us.

"I trust you found the little present I left for you on the desk?" he asks while sipping from a cold bottle of Cairo beer.

The bar is busy for so early in the morning. At least three men are bellied up to it, slow drinking beer and liquor. One is dressed in a bush jacket and heavy boots. He's sporting long black hair that's tied back in a ponytail. His skin is browned from the sun and covered in a sheen of desert sand, which tells me he hasn't been in the city for very long. Another shorter, stockier man is dressed in light leather coat which is also weathered by the sun, like my own. He's wearing a fedora that's seen its fair share of desert sand and sun. Another, an Arab, is wearing a dark business suit, and he's compulsively checking his smartphone. I'm keeping one eye on all three of them, the other on Sameh and Anya.

"Found it," I answer Sameh. "All one-point-six pounds of it. Fully loaded."

I hand one of the whiskeys to Anya. I lift mine.

"Cheers," I say.

We drink.

"But this isn't the time to celebrate," I say, setting my empty glass back down on the bar. "We have an archeologist to find."

Anya sets her now empty glass back down on the bar.

"Where to?" Sameh asks, lifting his car keys from off the bar.

"I'll let you know on the way," I say, giving the three men another glance over my right shoulder before about-facing and making for the exit.

Driving.

Zipping our way in and out of a series of seemingly never-ending alleys. Until we come to a section of road located under a highway overpass. No space goes unutilized in Cairo, a city supporting a population larger than Los Angeles, but boasting only half the land. In this case, a bustling market has been created by the addition of the overpass. The market runs the entire length of highway construction.

I tell Sameh to stop outside a series of small shops that serve as the market's unofficial entrance. The shops are nothing more than shacks that have been assembled out of scrap wood and tin.

"I'll be right back," I say, hopping out of the front shotgun seat.

"I'm coming," Anya insists.

"Wait for me here," I demand, closing the door, knowing that what lurks inside that maze of people, animals, food, and goods is danger. It's easy to get lost inside this marketplace and even easier to be snatched up by someone who has their eye out for you.

I run off before she gets the chance to change my mind.

Disappearing into the crowd of gawkers and spice sellers, I enter into the marketplace. Barefoot men dressed in robes and headdresses hound me to enter into their stores to buy their spices or jewels. Hopeless barefoot cripples beg for coins. Pot-and-pan sellers take hold of my arm, try and force me to behold the workmanship on their metal cookware. Bread bakers pull thin little freshly baked loafs from the coal-fired ovens with long-handled paddles and deposit them onto blankets laid out on the road to cool. The black burka-wearing women line up obediently to purchase the bread for the mid-day meal. Farther in are the rug and Egyptian cotton merchants. Not far up ahead of them, the knife and sword stores. Beyond them, the butcher shops, their windows filled with cow heads, newly amputated hoofs and extracted stomachs. The flies gather around the newly butchered meat and make their home in its congealed blood. The odor of the sunbaked meat is so rotten and pungent, I'm forced to breathe through my mouth and not my nose.

The shop I want is located on a less traveled

walkway set perpendicular to this one. I hook a right at the corner and follow the less dense, awning-covered path until I come to a golden elephant. The elephant is as large as I am. Set beside it, is a wooden camel. The camel is also big and must weight five hundred pounds having been carved out of pure cypress over a century ago. In between the two animals is the shop entrance. I open the glass and wood door to the ping-ping-ping sound of a little brass bell that hangs off the door's interior. The old fashioned bell serves as a kind of alarm. It rings whenever the door is opened or closed.

Closing the door behind me, I lock it. I grab hold of the wood sign that hangs from a nail embedded into the top of the door frame and turn it around so that the word CLOSED, stenciled in both English and Egyptian Arabic, faces the marketplace, while the word OPEN faces the shop's insides.

"Can I help you?" comes a voice from far back in the shop's interior.

The short, portly, gray-mustached shopkeeper emerges from a space filled to capacity with antique tables, chairs, marble statues of Egyptian Gods and Goddesses, sarcophagi, mummies, coffins, mummified animals, half-moon shaped swords, gilded mirrors, and more. At first, he doesn't know what to make of his open/closed sign. Until he spots the man who's messed with it.

He assumes an ear to ear smile that is about as unauthentic as half the unlicensed junk displayed inside a shop that passes itself off as a home for priceless Egyptian artifacts and antiquities for the discerning private collector.

"Chase Baker!" he shouts as if with joy. "Well why did you not tell me you were coming by for a visit? How long have you been back in the land of the living?"

He pulls out a white handkerchief and begins to wipe his brow.

I pull the 9mm from my pant waist, aim it at his head.

"You still have something that belongs to me, Amun."

In my head I'm picturing the missing half mirror that's identical to the half mirror housed inside my right pocket. A mirror that I dug up in the desert not far from here, but that Amun illegally purchased off one of my laborers after the boy lifted it from out of my tent one night while I was sleeping off a bender. Amun and I both know he purchased it for nothing from the laborer, but I have no way of getting it back from him short of shooting him in the head. And the punishment for a white westerner shooting a Muslim in the head in Cairo is not pleasant considering it will involve a long and drawn out torture which will climax with my public beheading.

Amun sports a thick black mustache and he is dressed in his usual white suit which is far too small for his middle-aged girth. He's the type of man who would wear a bright red fez on his head if the fashion didn't die out with the city's modernization back in the late sixties and seventies. A modernization that has since faded and crumbled into history along with the rise of the Muslim

Brotherhood and a tighter than tight rein on all things perceived as a threat to Islamic law.

"I assure you, Chase," he says in a half-whisper, "I would never be so bold as to acquire anything of yours without paying a fair price." He smiles, wipes the sweat from his brow. "Anything else would be stealing."

"Stealing is the perfect word for it," I say, my pistol now aimed point blank for his round belly. "But I might be willing to go easy on you if you give me some information."

He shakes his head.

"Information? About what?"

Slowly, I begin making my way towards him, all the time roaming the goods on display with my eyes.

"There's a dig going on in the desert outside the Giza Plateau. Probably to the west of it. Some wealthy members of the new regime might be sponsoring it. The lead archeologist is a friend of mine. He was teaching in Florence for a while until suddenly ... poof ... he vanished into thin air. There's some talk that he might have been kidnaped by said wealthy regime members, and that these men are willing to go to extreme measures to acquire a very rare artifact. An artifact that my friend has been searching for, for a good many years. Sound familiar?"

More wiping of the brow. More smiling.

"I haven't the faintest idea. Digs are going on all the time. You know that, Chase. You've worked on many of them yourself. So did your father." He issues me a brown-nosing smile. "You were one of the best sandhogs around. Until you traded in your shovel for a typewriter."

I thumb back the hammer on the 9mm, raise my aim so that it's pointing at his head.

"Maybe I can somehow convince you to think harder. I'm sure you keep a running tally of every single dig going on from Cairo to the Libyan border."

He swallows something hard, his Adam's apple bobbing up and down inside his neck like a turkey about to face the hatchet.

"Well, it's possible that knowledge of the dig you're talking about has come to my attention."

My eye catches something over his shoulder. Something displayed up on a shelf behind a long, glass case, like the kind jewelers use in their stores. It's a box. A box carved out of sandstone, with a gabled top. It's an ossuary. Like the kind Dr. Manion might dig up in his quest to find the bones of Christ. Dig up while a gun is pointing at the back of his head …

I wave the gun in the direction of the ossuary.

"That's a nice piece you have up there. From my vantage point, I'd say that is an ossuary favored by first century Jews. Might be precisely the kind of thing my friend has been digging up out there in the desert."

He forces another smile, shakes his head.

"Chase, you're confusing me."

The gun back on his head.

"Where's the dig, Amun?"

He swallows again, and begins back-stepping towards the glass counter. He becomes startled

141

when his fat back end hits the counter unexpectedly. Turning, he goes around to the business side of the counter and once more faces me.

"Tell me, Amun. Tell me now. My index finger is getting very, very heavy. I wouldn't want it to suddenly drop down onto the trigger."

He's not bothering to wipe the sweat from his forehead now, allowing the streaks to run down his cheeks.

Using my good hand, I pull the map of the Giza Plateau and the desert beyond it from the interior pocket of my jacket. I lay it out onto the glass counter.

"Show me the location," I press.

He hesitates.

I press the gun barrel hard against his forehead.

"Show me now."

More swallowing, his heavy body trembling.

There's a pencil/pen jar set out on the counter beside a pad of paper. The writing tools are for potential buyers who feel more comfortable and far less vulnerable haggling over price without the ambiguity of spoken language. I grab a pencil, put it into his hand.

"Use this."

He holds the pencil in his hand and for a brief moment, just dangles it over the map.

"Now!" I shout, raising up my pistol, shooting a round into the old ceiling-mounted Casablanca fan that hangs from the ceiling. Shards of wood and plaster drop down onto the glass counter. But the shot serves to grab his undivided attention.

"Please," he says, holding up his chubby hands

142

in surrender. "You need not become violent."

He presses the pencil down on an area that's maybe twenty or twenty-five miles outside the Giza Plateau in the direction of Libya.

"Mark it," I say, once more pressing the now smoking barrel against his moist forehead.

He makes an X and tosses the pencil.

Sometimes X does indeed mark the spot...

"Are you happy, Chase?" he begs, his voice so angry I fear he might cry. "Are you happy now that my life is in danger? You come here for a short time, demanding things from me that I am not at liberty to give you. That I don't owe you. If certain members of the new government should find out about this, I am as good as dead. They will come for me in the night while you are sleeping peacefully in your bed in Florence. Or New York."

"I'm hoping for New York, Amun. Hoping to see my daughter again. And I don't give a shit if you live or die." Manually thumbing back the pistol hammer. "Now while we're at it, the mirror."

"Please, Chase," he cries. "We had an agreement. You asked me for information and I gave it to you. Please ..."

"You also have the other half of my mirror and I want it back."

A doors opens. Not a front door, but a door in back. Then the sound of footsteps. Heavy, thick-soled boot-steps. A glance over my shoulder reveals two men entering onto the floor. I recognize the men. They are two out of the three men who were drinking at the King's Hotel bar just moments ago. The pony-tailed one wearing the bush jacket and the built one in the black leather jacket and fedora. Eyes wide, they come at me, drawing their side-arms.

"Now would be a good time to remove your weapon from my forehead, Chase," Amun whispers gently, that sly smile having returned to his fat mustached face. "And while you're at it, please get down on your knees and prepare yourself for a burial in the desert."

22

Slowly, I lower the pistol.

While I'm doing it, I gaze down into the glass. It was right in front of me the entire time. A small mirror, about the size of my palm. One side of it is jagged from having been broken off from the identical half-mirror I'm now carrying in my right trouser pocket.

"Drop the gun," the first, pony-tailed man insists. By the sounds of it, he's an American. He cocks the hammer on his revolver.

"Do it," demands his partner. A man who is most definitely Egyptian. "Or we won't hesitate to shoot you here and dispose of your body in the desert."

"Don't I know you fellas?" I say.

I lower the 9mm, go to set it onto the glass counter. But, rather than set it gently, I swing the barrel down hard, shattering the glass.

Pony-Tail shoots, misses, the bullet shattering the storefront window.

Amun screams, drops to his knees beside the glass counter.

I point the 9mm at the two goons, depress the trigger, fire at will. I hit the heavier one in the chest. He drops like an obelisk onto the floor while Pony-Tail runs for cover behind an upright wood Pharaoh's coffin.

I reach down into the counter, grab the mirror and the map, stuff them both into my pocket while the rounds from Pony-Tail's revolver whizz by my head.

"I'll be seeing you in all the filthy places, Amun," I shout, as I make a flying leap out the shattered storefront window.

23

I land on my right side just as a donkey is trotting past, pulling a wood cart behind it.

I roll my body under the cart and, emerging out the opposite side, get back up onto my feet at the very same moment Pony-Tail starts shooting at me from out of the shattered storefront. People scream, scatter about in every direction. It's the kind of confusion and cover I need as I make an all-out sprint for the center of the market.

I don't get far before I make out another shot and sense a round shooting past my right ear. I duck into a shop that sells rugs, take a quick glance over my shoulder.

Pony-Tail is coming at me down the center of the narrow road, the Arabs moving out of his way, like he owns the place. Thumbing the clip release, I allow the metal clip to drop to the store floor. I reach into my jacket pocket, pull out a fresh one, slap it home.

The store owner is jabbing at my back. He wants me to leave his store. He doesn't care that I'm holding a loaded gun. I reach into my left-hand pocket, pull out some Egyptian pounds, toss them at him. Then, sucking down a breath, I jump back out into the street.

I aim the gun at Pony-Tail.

There's a shot. He drops to his knees, then onto his face.

I look one way and the other. With all the people scattering all about, screaming and shouting for help, I can't make out who did the shooting.

Until she reveals herself.

Anya.

"Got your back, Ren Man," she says, smiling.

She runs to me.

"Question is," I say, "who's got yours?"

I don't have time for an answer before I hear the wail of sirens and the screeching of truck tires.

"Where'd you get the gun?" I ask her while we make a sprint for Sameh's car.

"Our fixer is very fixed," she shouts in between breaths. "He's helping me protect my investment."

"Should have guessed," I say. Then, as Sameh pulls up in front of us, breaking the car so hard it fishtails on the gravelly road, "I think I know where your husband is."

I open the door for her.

She jumps in.

I go around, get into the front.

"Drive," I say to Sameh.

"Where to?"

"Just point the car towards Libya," I say. "And don't stop."

24

"We need better transport," I say to Sameh, as he weaves in and out of the slow moving vehicles, making his way to the above-ground highway that will lead us some of the way to the Giza urban interior.

"What do you suggest we do?" he says. "Go car shopping?"

"Cairo's too hot. We need something that will take us into the desert. A four-by-four. A truck, van, suburban ... Something, anything. But not this."

"Hold onto the wheel," Sameh instructs.

"What? In this traffic?"

"Just hold the wheel please, Chase. Traffic is light today."

This is what he calls light?

I reach over and do it. He's still got his foot on the gas, so I'm doing my best to avoid smashing into the slower moving cars that we are constantly tailing. Using only my left hand, I turn the wheel to the right, then back to the left, then straight, then a quick right again. I feel like I'm caught inside a real action, real-time video game. Meanwhile Sameh searches his cell phone for a number. When he finds it, he speed-dials the number, takes back the wheel.

"Thank you, Dario Franchitti," he says, not without a smile. Sameh the jokester. Somehow I imagine a world famous pro auto racer like Mr. Franchitti has an easier time winning the *Indianapolis 500* than he would negotiating the roads of Cairo. But then, what the hell do I know?

"Yes, thank you, Dario for scaring the living crap out me," Anya scolds from the back seat. She is not smiling. If she possessed an Adam's apple, it would be bobbing up and down inside her neck.

We make it to the highway, and Sameh guns the sedan up the entry ramp. For the first time since we started driving, we enjoy a relatively open road. He presses the pedal to the floor while, with his cell phone pressed to his right ear, he speaks something loud in Arabic.

I shoot a glance at Anya. She shoots me a tentative look back.

With my eyes back on the road, I see the many people who line the shoulder of this three-lane highway. They're waiting for anyone who might decide to play taxi cab driver and, for a price, stop alongside the road and give them a ride. There seems to be no shortage of people who are willing to carry passengers for money, as the cars and pickup trucks randomly pull off to the side. Some of them do it without warning, so that Sameh must skillfully veer to the left in order to avoid smashing into them as they brake and decelerate without warning.

Maybe three minutes pass of this reckless, almost suicidal driving until the sun-soaked horizon changes into something remarkable. The red-orange ball of sun is no longer alone as it kisses the tops of three pyramidal stone structures.

The pyramids of Giza.

I've been in the presence of the pyramids a few times before. I could say that they still take my breath away. Or that they fill me with awe and wonder and excitement. But these are weak pedestrian descriptions. Truer to say that whenever I am in the presence of the ancient pyramids at Giza, I feel slightly uncomfortable. Like I would with a girlfriend or a wife who is truly beautiful, truly well-constructed, amazingly intelligent, but who nonetheless possesses secrets which she greedily guards. And for this reason, no matter how much I love her, I will never fully trust her.

Anya sits up, pokes her head between the opening between the two front seats.

"I've only seen them in pictures and in film," she whispers to no one in particular, as the three pyramids take on more form and no longer become a part of the horizon, but the horizon itself.

"Take a good look," I say. "Because there lies our's and your husband's future, should we luck out and actually find him."

"Alive," she says, setting her hand on my arm. "Don't forget the alive part."

"Yes," I nod. "Very much alive ... Let's hope."

Sameh pulls up to a garage with an old-fashioned gas pump mounted to a concrete pad out in front of it. My guess is the pump no longer does the job it was originally intended to do so many decades ago. But the automotive garage certainly is. There are two bays, both of which are occupied with vehicles set up on hydraulic risers. With the overhead doors opened, I can make out the teams of robed Arabs tending to the undersides of the two vehicles. Leaning against the old brick building are all sorts of automotive parts, from exhausts to full engines. Set beside those is a pile of used tires.

A man comes out to greet us. He's tall, slim, dressed in blue jeans and a light button-down shirt. He's wiping grease from his hands with an oil-stained rag as he comes around to the driver's side of the sedan. I take him for the garage owner and the man Sameh was talking with on the cell phone earlier. He and Sameh greet one another with the usual, "As-salam alaykum," which means, "Peace be upon you" as much as it does, "Hey, what's up?"

While the two men exchange a few more words, the garage owner picks at his black goatee and takes occasional glances at myself and Anya. After a minute or two of this, Sameh turns to me.

"This man's name is Nisbah. He can provide us with a Toyota Land Cruiser. A 1979 model which is greatly favored in the desert. More so than newer models."

In my mind I picture the boxy-looking but fully functional four-by-four, since I've driven them more times than I can count.

"Precisely what we require," I say. "And a full tank, plus four extra cans of gasoline."

"Nisbah will provide what you need for your journey into the desert. However, he will accept only cash. Trust is a commodity these days in post-revolutionary Egypt."

Pulling out the pile of cash from my trouser pocket, I pose, "How much?"

"Three hundred dollars," Sameh says. "U.S. dollars."

"I have plenty of Egyptian pounds," I say, holding them up.

The goateed Nisbah shakes his head, waves the pounds away like they smell of skunk.

"Egyptian pounds are no good to him," Sameh explains. "They are not worth the paper they are printed on in this the day of the new Pharaohs."

"I understand," I say. "But I have only pounds and Euros, since I haven't been back to the States in some time." Then, to Anya. "How much cash do you have?"

She reaches into her bag, produces a small wallet. She comes back out with three, crisp one hundred dollar bills. She holds them up.

"Will this do?"

"Thanks for holding out on us, money bags," I say, snatching them from her hand and, reaching across Sameh, handing them directly to Nisbah.

He nods, smiles.

"Pull in, please. Your ride awaits you. So does the unrelenting Egyptian desert."

He laughs so hard when he backs away from the car, I think he might double over. But nothing is funny about the desert. It is dead land, and only the dead thrive there.

25

An hour later we are driving along a narrow road that borders the perimeter of the Giza Plateau and the Great Pyramids. Sameh is behind the wheel of a white Toyota Land Cruiser that's been stocked with food, water, weapons, night vision gear, sleeping bags ... you name it. Everything you need for survival in the desert which just might include staying alive during a potential shootout with some nasty radical Muslim bandits bent on stealing the remains of the Christian Messiah.

I ride shotgun while Anya occupies the safer back seat, directly behind Sameh. She has her window down and she seems mesmerized by the pyramids as we pass them by on a gently inclining sand-covered road that leads to nowhere but wide open desert.

On our way around the pyramids we pass by

camels and donkeys and the Arab jockeys who ride them and offer the beasts up to the scattering of tourists for rides. Robed beggars walk barefoot in the sand while gawkers try to push what they refer to as traditional Arab headdresses. They sell mini-pyramids and small colorful square beads said to be magic treasure uncovered in the tombs. But in reality it is all junk intended as cheap souvenirs for the hordes of tourists who flock here annually.

Used to flock here, I should say.

Nowadays only a fraction of the multitudes of tourists make their way to this land of violent change and upheaval. Something that on one hand is tragic for the vendors and gawkers, but for our purposes, will be to our benefit, since we will require the Third Pyramid all to ourselves. Once we locate Andre, that is.

We head off-road, on into the desert just as the sun begins to set over the western plain. As darkness approaches an hour later, Sameh brings the Land Cruiser to a stop.

"We will camp here for the night," he informs. "It is too dangerous to travel at night. The pirates are everywhere. We stand the chance of being ambushed. Better to settle in for the night and continue at sun up. Agreed?"

"Agreed," I say.

"Agreed," adds Anya. Then, "Sameh, if you build us a fire, I will prepare a feast."

"Exactly what I want to hear, miss," he says, hopping out of the truck and immediately going about the work of setting up a campsite.

I pull out my 9mm, thumb the clip release, check

and recheck the nine-round load.

"I'll make a check on the perimeter," I say, grabbing the pair of Bausch & Lomb night-vision binoculars set on the dash.

Exiting the four-by-four, I proceed out into the desert on foot.

I trek in a westerly direction, towards the setting sun.

The heat from the desert is quickly fading as the sunlight begins to diminish into what will be a darkness so absolute, the stars in the sky will appear close enough to touch, as if they were white Christmas lights dangling from a black ceiling. Lifting the binoculars to my face, I scan the horizon for anything that might appear to be out of the ordinary. Anything that's moving.

I see nothing but sand dunes for as far as the lenses can magnify. But then, that's not entirely true. As the sunlight quickly fades and the green hue-like night vision begins to operate on the binoculars, I start to make out something that looks like ghosts dancing on the horizon. Swirling shapes that swiftly twist and turn their way up, down, and across the dunes. But they are not ghosts. They are tornado-like pillars of loose sand being sucked up by the wind. An ever increasing wind.

I remove the binoculars and contemplate the meaning of the wind.

I know that if it should get any worse, we could easily find ourselves trapped in the middle of a sandstorm. I've never actually been caught up in one, but through the years, I've met archeologists and sandhogs who have. Rough, tough types who take crap from no one or anything. Men and women who don't scare so easily be it a jet plane that blows an engine mid-flight or waking up to a scorpion crawling on their face in the middle of the night. But when they spoke of the desert consuming them in a windstorm powered by hurricane-force winds, their faces took on a chalk-white pallor and their eyes a curious deadness, as if they were recounting their bloody experiences in combat.

Those ghosts I just witnessed way out there in the desert distance … I'm hoping they remain just ghosts and that we are in for a peaceful night, or the last thing any of us will have to worry about is finding Manion or the Jesus remains. If a sandstorm blows through, it will be our very lives that will hang in the balance. By this time tomorrow night, we could become a fixture of the desert. A permanent fixture buried in sand like some undiscovered Pharaoh or even Jesus Himself.

About-facing, I follow my footsteps back to camp, knowing that for now anyway, we are all alone in this vast, desolate wilderness and the only visible enemy looming on the periphery, is the wind.

26

After dinner we slip into our sleeping bags which have been positioned around the deadwood fire. Sameh begins to snore almost immediately, even though the wind is noticeably increasing in velocity.

If he's not frightened, then why should I be?

Anya and I stare into the fire, sharing occasional sips from a pint of whiskey I stowed away for myself after purchasing it off a back alley contraband vendor in Giza while the Land Cruiser was being tended to—a shop that also sold thick black bricks of Afghan hash.

"How do you think he'll react when you first see him?" I say.

"How will who react?" Anya says, bits of her thick brown hair blowing in the wind.

"Your husband, Andre. He's liable to have no idea that you're looking for him."

I watch her cock her head while pulling herself tighter into her sleeping bag, her beautifully tanned face aglow in the firelight.

"You're right, Ren Man," she says in a half-whisper, while staring into the flames. "I'm the last person he'd expect to see out here."

"You mean you're the last person he'd expect to see trying to save his skinny ass."

She turns to me, smiles.

"Bingo," she says. "We didn't part on particularly terrific terms."

"But you have, in fact, parted ways," I stress.

She nods, the flame from the fire reflected in her eyes.

"But you know that already, Chase. Do you want me to produce divorce papers for you?"

"Do you still love him?"

More nodding.

"You mean, like do I love him in the take-him-back-and-try-again sense of the L word?"

"Yes, that."

"Not a chance. We tried plenty of times and plenty of times it didn't work. No matter how good we looked together on paper ... The English professor and the archeology professor together forever, surrounded by adoring students, living in the perfect little picket-fenced house located on the perfect spec of property just outside the college campus ... It all sounds nice and romantic, but it just didn't work. He's too married to his buried antiquities and the distant past, and I'm too married to loneliness-in-the-present-and-future tenses."

"But you still love him enough to find him."

"Yes, I will always care for him and his well-being. But I will no longer be *in love* with him. There's a distinct difference."

The foreboding wind picks up, fanning the flames. I feel some of the harsh sand against my face.

"Winds beginning to blow," Anya says, a noticeable hint of fear on her flame lit face.

"So I'm aware. I've been paying some attention to it."

She glances over Sameh's way.

"He doesn't seem too worried about anything. He's sleeping like a baby."

I too gaze at the sleeping Sameh. He's lying on his back, snoring, mouth open, catching sand flies.

"That's a good thing," I add. Then, as if using Sameh's loud snores as my cue, I steal another sip of whiskey from the bottle, cap it off, and shuffle out of my sleeping bag, snaking my way over the now compacted sand to Anya.

"Excuse me?" she whispers. "But nuns and priests are forbidden to fornicate with one another."

"I've forever lost the collar. And I've heard rumors about you leaving the order, sister. How shocking."

Whiskey pint in hand, I climb into her bag, feet first, feel myself rubbing up against her soft but somehow hard body, feel the heat from the fire on the back of my head and neck, feel the wind that's blowing and whispering its way across the endless dunes.

"This isn't the writer collecting new material for a new Chase Baker mystery novel is it?" Anya begs.

"Promise," I say, crossing my heart. "I find it sexy that you've read my books, teacher."

Pursing her lips.

"Maybe one or two. Not exactly the stuff I would recommend to college advisory board as required reading for English lit majors."

"Now that hurts."

"But not bad. You have a terrific sense of economy of language and you are a pile driving plotter. How's that for kind critiquing?"

"Keep spreading it," I say. "If you'll pardon my pun."

She kicks me inside the sleeping bag.

"You're a devil, Ren Man," she giggles. "But in all seriousness, I can tell you write the way you live, which is not entirely without danger."

"Our world expands or shrinks in direct proportion to our courage," I say, stealing another sip from the bottle.

"No truer words. But then, you are not a very domestic character, Mr. Baker. Not the nine-to-five, hearth-and-kettle kind of dad and husband."

I shake my head.

"Suburbia is a prison. I get cabin fever too easily."

"But that's no excuse not to go back to your wife and daughter."

"It's far too late for that, Anya ... What I mean is, I miss my daughter. Part of why I'm doing this is so I can go back to New York to see her again. But as far as my ex goes, it's long over."

"Has she remarried?"

I'm not sure why, but the mere mention of my ex

being remarried feels like a punch in the gut.

"She hooked up with an investment banker who owns a townhouse on Gramercy Park in the city. He's a great provider. A great stepdad to my daughter. Home seven nights a week and always available for PTA meetings."

"But that's not your cup of whiskey."

I stare into the fire for a bit as if it's possible to see my past and all the mistakes of my past inside the flickering flames. I swallow another drink from the pint knowing that the booze will help me forget.

"I have a confession to make, sister," I say after a time. "I had always thought that I would marry the love of my life, and together we'd see the world, have a child along the way, share adventures, never staying in the same place for too long."

She's already biting down on her lip before I'm done talking.

"Women don't want that, Chase. Most women anyway. Women want stability. Security." She steals a moment for the thought to sink in. "You know what? I can bet your ex-wife still loves you very much. Kind of like I still love Andre. Only she knows she can't be with you."

"How's that?"

"A man like you, Chase, you're never satisfied. You're never comfortable in one place at one time. You can be sipping coffee outside the Eiffel Tower on a beautiful sunny day in April with not a worry in the world, but you will be consumed with nagging thoughts on where to go next before too much life runs out. Am I right?"

"No comment."

She giggles.

"You know I'm right. This might hurt, but the best thing for your wife is to have this new man in her life. A man like you, Chase…You're handsome, full of energy, talented at many things. You're the true Renaissance man…You see life as this great adventure. But when it comes to being a good husband and a good dad, you are a perfect poison."

The fire flares up in the wind gusts.

"Is that what I am? Poison?" Raising my head up. "But I love them. With all my heart."

"And they know that you love them. They can feel it from afar. Perhaps they even prefer to feel your love from afar. It's like feeling the sun on your face after a long winter, but don't look directly into it."

We watch the flickering fire for a while longer. Then, after a time, Anya shifts herself closer to me. Or, as close as she can come without being on top of me.

"Kiss me, Ren Man," she says. "Forget about the past, just for a little while, and be here now."

She unbuttons her shirt, kisses me on the mouth hard and sweet, our tongues touching, playing. Placing her hand on my head, she gently pushes me down onto the sweet spot between her breasts, shifting herself so that her right breast enters into my mouth. I suckle her erect nipple with my tongue, lips and teeth.

I feel her hand sliding down inside the tight space created by the sleeping bag, until she finds my belt. Almost skillfully she manages to unbuckle it, while proceeding to unbutton and unzip my pants. Reaching inside, I feel the good warm feel of her hand sliding down the length of my hardness before ever so gently pulling all of me out. I find my hand sliding into her pants, then into her silky lace panties, my fingers gliding over a soft tuft of trimmed hair until they find their home inside her soft, warm, wetness.

She's breathing hard now, her heart pounding against my own, our tongues and lips connected and never still. In the womb-like fit of the sleeping bag, she manages to spread her legs just enough for me to enter into her. We move steadily, slowly, but hard in the new gusts of wind and the flashing of the flames. Until we gradually go faster and faster and never ending, the wind blowing across the desert and against the orange flames and our hearts beating so rapidly I can hear the pounding in my temples and the tightness in my chest, and her breathing now turned to moans and sighs as we reach that place where we both release at the same time, and she is in me and I am in her.

The wind picks up yet again, sparks from the fire cascading up into the dark, desert sky. Together we hold each other tightly, sweetly, protectively. It's as if we will never let go.

That's how we fall asleep in the Egyptian desert. In one another's arms, to the wind, to the fire, to our separate memories and painful recollections. To Sameh's snores.

To our beating hearts.

27

We wake to the wind. A violent, gale force wind, blowing at us from out of the east. Just like I knew it would when observing the wind ghosts the night before.

Hard pellets of sand and hot sparks from the dying fire sting my face and eyes. The night has given way to dawn, but the dark cloud cover blocks almost the entirety of the brilliant sunlight. Anya screams, but the howling wind nearly silences her completely.

I slide out of the bag and fall flat onto my back from a gust of wind that feels more like the charging tackle of an NFL linebacker. I try and shield my eyes while forcing my feet back into my boots and desperately searching the immediate area for Sameh. That's when I make out an object coming at me from over my left shoulder. The two headlights piercing the sand-filled wind give the object away. The Land Cruiser comes to a stop, and I see a figure emerge from behind the wheel.

Sameh.

He's got a keffiyeh wrapped around his face and military-style goggles protecting his eyes. He grabs Anya by her jacket collar, begins to pull her up and out of her bag. Understanding what he is trying to do, I grab hold of her boots with one hand and assist him with the other. As soon as we are able to get her back up on her bare feet, the sleeping bag blows away in the wind, as if it bears no more weight than a common plastic grocery bag. Together, we stumble along across the ever-shifting sand pulling on Anya, trying with all our strength to move her to the safety of the Land Cruiser.

The rushing, jet-like wind pounds our bodies, but we somehow manage to get the back door open on the SUV. Working with one another, we toss Anya into the back seat, head first. Using hand signals, I let Sameh know that I am going around to the shotgun seat. He nods and, pulling open the driver's side door, shoves himself back behind the wheel.

Once inside with the doors shut, I swallow a deep breath.

"The Gods must really be pissed off today," Anya says, coughing up sand from her lungs.

"We're tomb raiders," I say, fingering the sand out of the corners of both my eyes. "What the hell do you expect?"

"Thought you were here to save a life?" Anya questions. She's rapidly lacing up her boots now that she's got them back on her feet.

"Goes without saying."

"I have water," Sameh points out, reaching around back to hand Anya a plastic bottle. She takes it in her hand, drinks from it. Coughs and drinks. When she's got her breathing under control, she hands me the water. I take a deep drink, wipe my mouth with the back of my hand.

I stare out the windshield of a Toyota Land Cruiser that's bucking like a bronco in hurricane-like winds. Bucking so badly I'm fearing that we might tip onto our side. But I choose not to bring that possibility up in public. It's impossible to see even two feet beyond the glass, the wind is so fierce, the sand so thick.

I turn to our guide.

"Give it to me straight, Sameh. We gonna make it out of this shit storm?"

"Sandstorm," Anya corrects.

"Shit storm," I insist.

The guide cocks his head like, *Maybe yes, maybe no...*

Not the answer I want to see.

"Sameh," Anya interjects, while wiping sand from her leather jacket with her open hands, "what can we do to save ourselves?"

He pulls down his keffiyeh, runs his hands down his face.

"The best ... possible move ... right now ... is to stay right here," he says in between coughs intended to clear the sand from his throat. "Remain here, in the truck, and pray that it dies down in a few moments rather than three days from now." He clears his throat once more. "If that should happen, the desert will consume us entirely. Like the wrath of God."

Leaning over me, he presses his fingers against the dashboard vent, closes it. He proceeds to close all the vents in rapid succession. With the vents shut, the claustrophobic sensation of suffocating in our own stale air is all the more intense as the truck continues to buck violently, like an airplane caught up in severe turbulence.

"Chase, I'm scared," Anya reveals, reaching between the bucket seats for my left hand.

I hold her hand tight and for a time, all three of us sit helpless while the sand pounds the truck and the wind delivers her blow. It's then I make out the faint image of a cylinder. It's not instantly discernable against the blinding sea of brown sand that fills both my immediate line of site and my peripheries. But I know it's out there, coming towards us. Dancing, churning, destroying.

"Sameh," I say. "The binoculars."

He pulls his pair off his neck, hands them to me. I put them to my eyes and adjust the auto-focus. That's when I see the funnel cloud coming directly for us.

I hand the glasses back to Sameh.

"Twelve o'clock high," I say. "Tell me what you see."

He presses the binoculars to his eyes.

"For the love of Allah," he whispers.

"Can you drive us out of here?" I ask.

"Not a chance," he says, shaking his head. "We're blind, and even if I could start the engine we'd stall out immediately."

"What's happening?" Anya says, as the violent bucking becomes even more violent with the front end of the vehicle heaving up and down like a rearing and kicking bronco.

Sameh sets the binoculars down on the console.

"Anya," he says. "Lie down across the back seat, horizontally. Buckle your legs in with one seat belt and your torso in with the other. But make sure you face into the seatbacks."

"Why? What's going on? Why are we bouncing up and down?"

"Just do it," I shout, tightening my belt as tight as it will go.

Then comes the scream of the funnel cloud as it breaks through the sea of brown.

Anya screams as the Toyota lifts up trunk first and, like a stone that's tossed down steep a mountainside, begins to roll.

When I come to, the rolling of the truck has stopped. What had been a relentless howling dies down. The sunlight peeks its shining rays from out of the sand-filled clouds and daylight returns to the desert. The truck is back up on all four wheels, and the only visible sign of damage is a jagged crack in the windshield that stretches from the top driver's side corner all the way down to the passenger-side bottom corner. I'm not sure why but staring at it with my foggy head reminds me of staring at the jagged electronic line on a heart monitor.

"Allah is great," Sameh, says. "He has spared us our lives, and graced us with the good fortune of a very short storm."

"How long was I out?" I say.

"I was about to ask you the same thing," he says, checking his watch. Then, "No more than a minute judging by the time."

I unclasp my seatbelt, turn to get a look at Anya.

"You alive back there?"

She lifts her head up from where it was still shoved into the ninety-degree, L-shaped space between the seat and the seatback. Looking one way and then the other, "Nothing broken. What about you?"

I feel a pounding in my head. I can also make out a faint sound of bells ringing. I can recognize the effects of a slight concussion when I hear them. My skull must have slammed against the door panel when we rolled over in the sand. It's a bit bruised but nothing appears to be fractured which out here can mean death.

"All good, Anya," I say. It's not entirely the truth, but what the hell good will it do to complain. I'm sure Sameh is suffering from the same ringing in the head that I am. He goes to open his door, but there's so much sand built up on the opposite side, he must force it open with his left shoulder.

"Get out on my side," I say to Anya.

She unbuckles both belts and does it.

I open the door and slip on out into a desert that has transformed itself in only a few short, but somehow eternally long minutes. Where our camp once existed is now a small, wave-like dune. No trace of our fire is left over. Nor our sleeping bags. Not to worry. We have no plans for spending another night in the desert. That is if we can manage to extract Manion from his captors today. This very morning.

Sameh proceeds to examine the exterior of the Land Cruiser for any further damage that might have occurred. He walks around the vehicle, touching something here, kicking a tire there. When he's through he shoots me a look, and issues a thumbs up.

"No damage to speak of," he observes. "Lucky for us we rolled only two or three times on the soft sand. Allah is looking after us."

"You go with that, Sameh," I say. "Maybe you can ask him to work up a little coffee for us while he's at it."

"How about a Diet Coke instead, Ren Man," Anya offers, tossing me a lukewarm can she's retrieved from the back of the vehicle.

"That'll have to do," I say. Then to Sameh, while looking at my watch. "How much time you figure it'll take for us to reach Manion's dig? That is, the engine still runs?"

"We will pick up the desert road a few klicks from here," he says. "If it isn't too washed out with sand and debris, about one hour. A little more perhaps."

I crack open the Coke, take a deep drink, feel the carbonation against my throat, cutting through the layer of sand that seems to have embedded itself there. The caffeine that comes along with it, settles into my system, giving it a kick start.

"Then let's do this," I say.

We all file back into the Land Cruiser. Sameh crosses the fingers on his left hand while turning the engine over with the other. The engine fires back up.

"Toyota Land Cruiser 1979" he exhales. "There is no substitute."

He toe-taps the gas and pulls us out of a sand bank. After a few minutes we manage to locate a road that is partially covered in drifts of sand. He guns the heavy eight-cylinder and drives the desert road like the entire God fearing world depends upon it.

In a very real way, it does.

28

After an hour, Sameh takes us by surprise when he once more pulls off the road, begins heading across another seemingly forever stretch of wide open desert. The forever stretch is interrupted by a mountain range way off in the distance and in between it, a valley. I know these mountains to be constructed entirely of sandstone and Swiss-cheesed with thousands of caves, some long and large, others small and barely wide enough to fit a man should he crawl inside one of them on his belly.

The mountain range is deceiving.

What appears to be so close you can just about reach around and touch it, is really about fifty kilometers away. But that fifty klicks won't take us long to traverse with Sameh flooring it, pushing the Land Cruiser as hard as he can without risking a boil over in the ever elevating desert heat.

Another hour passes before he brings the truck to a stop at the base of a series of foothills that lead to the mountains, and kills the engine.

"We do the rest on foot in order to avoid a visible dust cloud from our tires," he says, turning to me. "If your information is correct, Chase, the dig will be one kilometer from here, on the other side of those hills."

I shoot Anya a look over my left shoulder.

"You good with this, boss? A klick is a little more than a half-mile."

"So long as you're good with it," she says. "And I'm not your boss, Ren Man."

"You're the bank. The bank is always the boss." I smile when I say it. But she doesn't.

We file out of the truck, gather weapons, ammunition, and other essentials including flares, rope, tape, binoculars, water, granola bars, first aid kit, keffiyehs, duct tape, sunglasses, two-way radios, pistols, grenades, two Ak47s with six extra banana mags, and a good old-fashioned, Soviet-made RPG with three warheads.

Sameh, guide of guides, comes prepared. But then, I'm certain that Checco had something to do with assisting in our supply of weaponry and survival gear.

Before we begin the trek, Sameh turns to us while pointing at the sunbaked hill directly before us.

"There is a trail that leads up through that hill," he says. "Once at the top we should have excellent cover with an even more excellent view of the valley beyond and the dig. Hopefully, we will spot

176

Dr. Manion alive and well."

"Hopefully," I repeat, adjusting the strap on my satchel bag so that it doesn't interfere with the AK47 and the RPG rounds I've elected to heft while Sameh straps the launcher to his back.

"He's okay," Anya says, her beautiful brown eyes now hidden behind a pair of Ray Ban Aviator sunglasses. "I can feel it." She too has been armed with an AK. Lucky girl.

"Let's move, Sameh," I insist, feeling the need to get moving while our employer's optimism lasts. "I want this to be a quick in-and-out job."

"Your wish is my command, good sir," he says, leading the way.

"Did he just say what I think he said?" I say to Anya.

"Your ears need no adjusting, Ren Man," she giggles.

I walk.

Like I've said before, distance in the desert is deceiving. So is the rate of vertical climb on what Sameh describes as a "hill." There's not a tree to be seen in this seemingly lifeless arid country, so the trail is really just a footpath that over the many centuries has been cut and carved into the sandstone with the sandaled or even bare feet of the many nomads that at one time or another throughout history, have called this inhospitable territory their home.

An hour of climbing passes before we're at the top of the hill. Almost immediately we make our way to the opposite site of the hilltop and look down upon the dig.

"Get down," I order, as all three of us collapse to our bellies. Bringing my binoculars to my eyes I make out a good-sized excavation which is going on outside the mouth of a cave. Behind it is a large tent that's been set up as a bivouac area. There's a 22 gauge rail-bed that's been set up at the mouth of the tent and that runs into the interior of the cave and no doubt goes for quite a distance inside the mountain. Parked beside the tent is a pair of 1990's era Toyota pickup trucks, one of which contains a tripod-mounted 30 cal. machine gun set in the bed.

God knows archeologists require the use of 30 cals...

Parked maybe fifty feet beyond the trucks is a helicopter. An old retrofitted Huey that must date back to the mid-1970s. The entire perimeter is surrounded by armed guards wearing the traditional headdress and light-weight, ankle-length kanduras or tunics of the Muslim Brotherhood. The white converse and Keds sneakers they choose for footwear make them look almost clownish. But I know these men to be steadfast in their beliefs and extremely lethal in their courage. The Japanese Kamikazes of World War Two have nothing on these would-be martyrs.

"You see him?" Sameh begs.

"Give me a sec," I say. "There's some people moving in and out of the cave. He could be one of them." Now handing the binocs to Anya. "You see him?"

She takes the binoculars in hand, sights in on the mouth of the cave for a few moments.

"That's him," she says. "In the green shirt and

the khaki hat … That's him … That's Andre."

"Allow me," I say, stealing the binoculars from her. Eyeing the cave, I see the green-shirted man. Dr. Andre Manion. He's a little bit thinner and grayer than the man I remember from eight years ago, but he is most definitely the same man. From my vantage point up on the hill, he appears to be arguing with someone who has not quite come into view since he is still hidden under the tent.

"What are you seeing?" Sameh poses.

"Hold onto your panties, Fixer," I say. That's when I see who Manion is arguing with. It's the suited man from the King's Hotel bar and the stocky, leather-jacketed goon who took a shot at me inside Amun's antique store. If the information Cip fed me back in Florence is correct, the suited man is an oil tycoon, and a very rich member of Cairo Muslim Brotherhood. He alone would possess the resources to sponsor a dig for the Jesus remains in the desert. He would also know of some interested buyers on the archeological black market once the bones are found. The suited man and his buddies must be choppering themselves in and out of the dig on a daily basis.

I roll over onto my side, face Sameh, hand him the binocs. I begin to explain about the suited man and the beefy leather-jacketed one. How they went after me at Amun's less than twenty-four hours ago.

Binoculars pressed against his eye sockets, he gazes at the two men in question, and exhales a long deep sigh.

"They are very bad people. Very wealthy and very powerful. If they get to us, they will kill us …

Behead us, more than likely. Do it on the internet for all the world to see. They will pretend to give credit to the Muslim Brotherhood or perhaps even Al Qaeda, and thus wash their hands of it."

"The only reason they haven't killed Manion is they need him," I suggest.

"How are we going to get him out of that hornet's nest without getting stung to death?" Anya inquires.

"How about we go all Bruce Willis on them," I offer. "Crash the joint, guns ablazin'."

I roll onto my side, face a nonresponsive Sameh and Anya.

"In all seriousness," I go on, "we've got two choices. We can try and bust up the camp now, starting with taking out those guards in broad daylight. Or, we can take the slow and methodical approach and hit them under the cover of darkness. It's your money Anya, and Sameh, it's your ass."

"Awfully dark in this desert at night," Sameh instructs. "We have night vision, but it's no guarantee that it will be effective should the wind decide to pick up again." He pauses for a minute to think. Then, "I'm sorry to say it, but we need to take him now. During the daylight." He smiles the smile of the optimist. "But I believe we can do it, Chase."

"Okay," I say. "We know what we're working with. It's too far for me to perform a flanking maneuver, so we'll have to go with the next best option."

"Which is?" Anya says.

"I'm going to politely walk right into their camp, and kindly ask them to release your husband."

29

Minutes later I have a 9mm strapped to my waist, another shoulder-holstered under my leather jacket. I have three grenades mounted to my leather belt and a fighting knife secured to my ankle with duct tape. Just for good measure, a pair of brass knuckles are resting at the ready inside my jacket pocket.

"You all know what to do," I say. "In exactly thirty minutes, we meet right back at this spot. All goes well, I will have Manion with me. If by some slim chance, I don't make it back here within one hour, don't wait any longer. Just go and live to rescue Andre another day. Understood?"

Anya nods like she's totally down with my plan. If you want to call it that. But I can smell the fear oozing off her body. Or perhaps the fear is my own. Doesn't matter. We just have to live with the fear, the same as we must live with the hot sun above our heads and the dry sand beneath out feet. Sameh raises up his right hand, rests it on my shoulder.

"Salem assalamu alaikum," he says. "You are my friend. Now, yallah. Go ... Yallah ... Go."

Turning back to Anya, I take hold of her arm, pull her into me, kiss her hard on the mouth. Pulling away, I say, "Wish me luck, baby."

"Don't get yourself killed, Ren Man," she says. "Heaven would bore you to death."

"And hell would never take me in."

With that, I begin descending the hill on its easterly slope so that I can maintain cover for as long as possible. I won't enjoy that cover for very long, but it's all I've got to work with. I also know that by the time I've reached the valley and begin making an all-out sprint towards the dig, Sameh and Anya will be keeping the armed bandits busy on the opposite side of the camp. That should leave me with only the suited man and his burly goon to deal with. In theory at least.

At the bottom of the hill, in the mouth of the valley, I pull out my hip-holstered, 9mm, cock a round into the chamber, thumb the safety off. What I wouldn't give right now for a horse. Or a camel. Maybe a motorcycle. But all I've got to rely upon are my legs. Legs that have seen better days.

Oh well, time to go to work...

Time to steal back my old boss, Dr. Andre Manion, and finally find the bones of Jesus of Nazareth, grab my ticket back to New York and my daughter. Sounds simple, right?

I run.

30

Small arms fire erupts from out on my left flank. One of the RPGs is triggered. I don't need to see it to recognize the sound I came to know so well during the first Gulf War. Its lethal warhead swooshes and sings a high-pitched song across the flat expanse of desert valley, takes out the interior of the chopper cockpit like a vengeful God on a bad day. A really, really bad day.

Good old, Sameh. Looks like he knows how to throw one hell of a party...

I sprint past the burning chopper feeling the heat from the flame while a half a dozen Muslim bandits shouting out Arabic curses focus their fire into the open valley in the opposite direction.

Ducking down before the first Toyota pickup, I see the suited man run out of the tent, followed by his leather-jacketed goon. Almost at the same time,

I see a man with a green shirt and a khaki hat emerge from the cave.

It's Manion.

"What in the Lord's name is happening?" Manion demands.

The suited, mustached man raises up his right arm, points an extended index finger at Manion.

"You ... You get back inside that cave!" he shouts in an Arabic accent. "This is no concern of yours. Yours is to work. To dig. To find what we've come for."

Small arms fires rattles our eardrums. It feels like the whole place is about to explode. But Manion doesn't go back inside the cave. He stands his ground while the gunfire grows more intense, fills the valley, echoing off the mountain and hillsides so that you never know precisely where the shooting is originating from.

I've got a clear choice here. I can take out both the business-suited man and his goon, leave them for buzzard food, snatch up Manion and head back to the rallying point, no worse for wear. Or, I can hold the suit and the goon at gunpoint, grab Manion and proceed to said rallying point without skipping a beat.

If I should go with the former, there's a good chance a bounty will be put on my head by some rather hateful religious fanatics whose arm extends far beyond the perimeters of the desert, Egypt, and even the Middle East for that matter. In a word, if I shoot these bastards where they stand in cold blood, their friends will stop at nothing to see me dead. They will come after me one night while I lie asleep in my bed in Florence or even New York. And once I'm dead, they could very well go after my daughter and my ex-wife. They might belong to the Muslim Brotherhood, but the rules of engagement apply in these matters. These people prefer to use swords for God's sake. Their preferred method of execution is beheading, just like it has been for thousands of years.

Better therefore that I opt for the latter choice, and at least present myself as somewhat chivalrous. Because this is indeed a crusade and, in the end, I'm only doing what they've already done: Stealing Manion. In the end, if I steal him back and uncover the true resting place of Jesus, all the better for me. I win, fair and square.

That solidly in mind, I raise myself up from my protective perch behind the pickup, aim the business end of the 9mm at the two captors.

"Down on your knees!" I shout.

Business suit shoots a look at the goon. He smoothes out his thick, black mustache with his forefinger and thumb like he's contemplating what sandwich to order from a MacDonald's menu. Leather Jacket mumbles something to his boss in Arabic. I haven't a clue what he's saying. But, if I had to guess, it would be something like, "Shall I kill this man now?"

Out the corner of my right eye, I'm watching Manion. The archeologist is staring at me, his jaw dropped to somewhere around the middle of his chest. I switch the pistol from my right hand to my left, never veering my aim from the two captors.

"Nice to see you again, Professor," I say. "Been

a long time. How's about a ride home?" He doesn't move. "Now, Professor. I ain't got all day and neither do you."

He drops what's in his hand, and approaches me.

In the distance, another explosion rocks the camp. I hear screaming. It's not the voice of Anya or Sameh. I'm guessing he's used his second RPG and scored a direct hit on a rat pack of bandits.

For a brief second, we all turn to gaze over our shoulders at the sight of the explosion. That's when Leather Jacket begins lifting his AK47, firing off a burst of rounds as the barrel raises up. It's all happening in slow motion, the rounds spitting up sand and gravel in a direct line for the spot of ground I occupy. I don't move now, I'll be split in two from caudal to clavicle.

Dropping fast onto my right-hand side, I trigger a volley of bullets that land square in the center of Leather Jacket's chest. He drops back onto his ass, speaks something soft and low, then lies back slowly, and dies. So much for trying to avoid a bounty on my scarred head.

I keep the gun poised on the suit.

"I know who you are," he says. "You have come for Jesus before, along with Dr. Manion. But you did not find him. Perhaps you know something now that I do not."

He smiles, as if I am going to share my secrets with him.

"What does a good old Muslim boy like yourself want with the bones of the Christian Christ?" I pose.

"The bones prove the Koran true. That Jesus, the mighty prophet, used an imposter to fill in for Him

186

on the cross. That the real Jesus married, bore children, lived a long life. When the world comes to realize the truth, the earth will shake and the heavens will open up and Allah will reveal himself as the true messiah. The true son of God."

"And, armed with this newly proven revelation, you and yours will no doubt declare a final war to end all wars with every Judeo/Christian on the planet. Am I close?"

Another smile.

"We shall proclaim ourselves victorious as Israel is crushed once and for all, and as the Vatican crumbles. You have seen your trade center destroyed and the thousands of infidels who burned and fell to their deaths. You have seen your ships and consulates attacked and obliterated with explosives. You have seen your people beheaded in the name of Allah on YouTube, and these things are mere preludes to a great and just war that is sure to come. Once we have the bones of Christ to prove the righteousness of our universal and ancient cause, nothing will stop us. Do you understand me, Mr. Chase?"

Now I feel the need to excavate the Jesus remains, not for the cash reward, or for the benefit of scholarly study, but simply to keep them away from the filthy hands of these radical extremists. Like I said, the God-fearing world depends upon it.

My pistol trembles in my hand.

It isn't as if it's grown heavy. More like its metal and plastic has come alive, its inner workings connected to the synapses in my brain and fueled by the anger in my heart I feel for this man and all he represents. But killing him like this is not my style. Wounding him might be a different story however.

Lowering my aim, I pull the trigger.

His right thigh explodes in a red spray of arterial blood.

Turning, I approach a stunned Manion. I grab hold of his arm.

"Let's go," I say.

Behind him, maybe two dozen robed workers fill the wide opening of the cave. Not a single one of them isn't smiling. My guess is that these workers are more or less slaves to the suited man. His cause. His threats of extremist style retribution should they protest their working conditions.

In the near distance, more gunfire.

Sameh is holding the bandits back, but I know it's only a matter of time until they come after me. Maybe a shorter time than I realize.

I spot the pickup with the 30 cal. mounted to it.

"There, Professor," I shout out to Manion. "You okay to drive?"

He nods. "Yes," he says. "I believe so, Chase."

I point to the opening in between the hills on the other side of the valley plain.

"I need you to take us through that pass. Gun it. Don't stop for anything until I tell you to. You with me, Professor?" He nods. "Good, now go."

We run for the truck. Opening the driver's side door, I pray the keys are in the ignition. Because this isn't Hollywood and I have no idea how to hotwire a Toyota pickup, or if it can be hotwired at all.

The keys are in the ignition.

Maybe Allah really is smiling down upon us...

"Fire her up, Professor!" I shout, as the bandits begin to give chase.

31

The pickup's thick off-road wheels spit up sand, until the four-by-four catches hold of firm earth. We buck forward heading in the direction of the pass just as the first shots whistle past my head.

Spinning the 30 cal. around on its tripod, I plant a bead on three bearded and robed bandits coming at me on horseback. The pale riders of my personal apocalypse. I thumb the trigger and spray them with multiple rounds. The first man's head explodes like a melon while the two behind him are split in half at the chest. The frightened horses stop, rear, turn and sprint off in the opposite direction of the gunfire. I don't expect them to stop running for hours.

For the moment there are no more bandits to be seen. But I know that more will be coming. In the meantime I take a quick visual survey of the surrounding landscape. I don't see Sameh anywhere. Pulling the radio from my belt, I make a call for him.

"Sameh, do you read me? Over."

Static fills the speaker as soon as I release the transmission trigger.

Thumbing the trigger again: "Sameh, do you read me? Sameh, you there? Over."

I listen for a response. But all I get is more static.

I don't have the time to make another call, because coming up on our tail is the second pickup. I aim for its front grill, trigger a short burst of belted 30 cal. rounds. The pickup engine explodes, a piston shooting out the metal hood like a ballistic missile. The truck spins out, comes to a dead stop. Two bandits emerge from the doors, firing their AK47s at us. But it's too late. We're already approaching the pass. I could shoot them, even from this distance. Shoot them out of anger, revenge. But I elect not to.

We've beaten the bastards already.

In broad daylight. Beaten them back.

It's only a matter of a few short hours until I come face to face with my maker and his remains. When that happens, it might be better if my conscience *and* my soul are clean.

32

Driving through the pass, I pound my fist against the pickup truck's metal roof, signaling Manion to stop at the designated rallying point which is located at the base of the hill.

He stops.

I look one way, then the other. Sameh and Anya are nowhere to be found. I pull my radio from my belt once more.

"Sameh," I speak into the transmitter. "Speak to me."

Releasing my thumb, I get nothing other than more static. Until the sound of static is broken by a voice. But the voice isn't coming from the radio. It's coming from on high.

I turn, look up.

Sameh is standing at the top of the hill, Anya right beside him.

"Coming down!" he shouts.

When he gets here, he shows me his radio which has been impaled with a bullet. He holds the palm-sized radio up like it's a sacred talisman.

"I am the luckiest man alive," he exhales. "The radio took a bullet meant for me."

I slap his back, knowing that Anya should have been equipped with a radio also.

"Thank Allah for small miracles," I say. Then, shifting my focus to Anya. "You okay?"

But she isn't looking at me. She is gazing into the eyes of her ex-husband.

"Hello Andre," she whispers in a hoarse voice no doubt choked with memory and desert sand.

"Hello Anya," he says. "I never…" He allows the thought to drop, as if the words need not be spoken. Truth be told, I'm feeling a little jealous of their reaction to seeing one another. What I sense is not hatred or indifference, but a man and a woman who genuinely care for one another. Two people who might even be surprised at their own reactions now that their physical separation has come to an end in the most unlikeliest of places.

"We should go," I say after a weighted moment. "The bandits will be coming after us as soon as they regroup."

"Everyone pile into the truck," Sameh says.

"I'm driving," I say. "Professor, you sit in front with me. We've got some talking to do. Sameh and Anya, you get on that 30 cal., case we need it."

"How do I work this thing?" Anya asks.

"Just point and shoot," I answer.

Without another word, I get behind the wheel,

start the truck up. After a few seconds, Andre opens the passenger side door, slips inside. He's as tall as I remember him, if not gaunt, with a graying beard and a face tanned to almost leathery proportions from constant exposure to the sun.

I shift the gear stick into first and begin the drive in the direction of our Land Cruiser.

"I know where the bones are buried, Professor."

He turns to me, quick.

"You saw the shroud," he says. "It's the only way you would know."

"I saw the shroud. And nearly got myself and your ex-wife killed in the process."

"They know."

"Who's they?"

"'They are everyone, everywhere. Everyone, everywhere who matters. Scholars, Rabbis, Priests, Imams … They all know about the mortal Jesus. The people who make religion. They are the real Gods. The people who guard the secrets of the past in order keep the money flowing in the present and in the future."

"People like the Vatican," I say.

"Belief in a divine Jesus is about control. Religion has always been about mortal man trying to make some sense of his existence. It's as instinctual as the need to breathe. The 'they' whom I talk about, feed on this instinct, and they gain a tremendous amount of power and money doing so. Most of our wars are fought over religious beliefs. Therefore, what might happen when you take one of the most steadfast beliefs away from them? The belief that Jesus rose from the dead on the third day ascended, physical body and soul, into paradise?"

"You crush them," I say. "And at the same time, empower other religions. Like Islam for instance. Radical Islam."

"The Jews don't believe in the divine Jesus," the professor adds.

"The Jews don't behead people."

"Neither do most Muslims. They are peaceful people who abhor those who tarnish the name of Allah with radical beliefs, hatred, and violent evil."

"But people will kill over what we are about to discover."

"Which is why our quest is so dangerous. Not to just our life and limb, but to the world. We have to be careful, Chase. If the bones of Christ are there to be found, it's our responsibility to find them. That's what I do. That's what I live for. It's why I exist."

"But what do we do if we really find them?"

I feel him looking at me. Driving over the bumpy, sand-packed terrain, I steal a glance over my shoulder, look into his deep-set eyes. I know then that he's not going to answer my question, because there is no real answer. Not yet. Because who can contemplate the profound moment that the body of Christ rests in your hands?

But then, after a time, he says, "Thank you for what you did back there."

"You're welcome. But I'm getting paid for this, and who knows, I might just get a good book out of it too, especially if we find the remains. For now, we need one another's help."

"Do you still have your half of the mirror, Chase?"

"I have both parts. And a CAD blueprint lifted from the shroud that dates back to 1978."

I can feel him smiling without having to look for evidence of it.

"Does Anya know about us? About our past?" he says. "About having worked together to find the bones once before."

"She knows some. But not everything."

"Such as?"

"She knows the part about me sandhogging for you. But not the part about me drinking my way into oblivion over a bad divorce."

"She trust you?"

"I think so," I say. "But she already suspects that I've been setting my sights on the Jesus remains from the get-go. But I somehow managed to convince her that in order to find you ... her ex-husband ... we first must find the path of the bones. That one would lead to the other."

"Brilliant," he says. "But what are your true motives, Chase?"

"You gotta ask?"

"You want to find the bones as much as I do."

"Can't help it," I say. "But when we do, we hand them to the right people. Not a private collector. Agreed? Those remains must be kept out of the hands of the extremists."

"Amen," he says. "Now, back up a bit and tell me how it is that you, of all people, have become my rescuer?"

"Long story," I say. And then I begin filling him in.

33

During what's left of the short drive over newly formed wave-like dunes of sunbaked desert back to the Land Cruiser, I fill Andre in on the highlights of what's transpired since I was nearly arrested back in Florence for balling my fist in the mout of a client whose wife had just balled me the night before.

"And now here we are," Manion says, as the Land Cruiser comes into view. "You and my ex-wife."

"Ex being the key prefix here, Professor."

He's quiet for a moment while we pull up on the Land Cruiser's tailgate.

"You having sex with my ex-wife, Chase?"

I steal a look at him while behind me, Anya and Sameh climb down from the bed.

"Let's put it this way, Professor," I say. "You're divorced and she's a free agent. Now that I've completed my mission and safely rescued you, I'm going to focus on finding the Jesus remains and I need you front and center to partner in the search."

Sameh knocks on the window.

"It's time to leave," he says through the glass.

"Coming," I say.

I feel Andre's hand on my leg.

"Chase," he says. "The shroud."

"What about it?"

"It's the third pyramid isn't it? The Menkaure's House of Eternity."

"Like you've always said."

"I would like to see the Shroud map as soon as possible."

"When I'm good and ready. And like I keep saying, it's not a map so much as a blueprint."

"Don't you trust me?"

"You ran out on me last time."

"You were drunk. Licking your wounds from a marriage gone bad. You were a mess. A dangerous mess. I needed a partner, not a drunk sandhog."

"Things have changed."

"I can see that."

Sameh waves at us to hurry along.

"Let's go," I say. "I'll tell you more on the way to the House of Eternity."

We make the transfer to the Land Cruiser. With Sameh back behind the wheel, Andre and Anya occupy the back seat. Before I assume my usual shotgun seat, I tell Sameh to wait one moment. Approaching the pickup truck with its mounted 30 cal., I pull a grenade from my belt, pull the pin. Holding down the arming mechanism with my thumb, I open the vehicle's driver's side door, toss the grenade in. As I jog my way back to the Land Cruiser, the grenade explodes, turning the pickup and the machine gun it houses into so much burning scrap metal.

Slipping back inside the Land Cruiser, I give Sameh the hand signal to go.

"Yallah," I say.

"Back to the Giza Plateau," he says.

34

The Third Pyramid of Giza is different from its two bigger siblings in several important respects, not the least of which is its far more solid construction. It's better built, as if its owner, the Pharaoh Menkaure, made a conscious decision to choose quality over quantity. Surrounding its entrance, which is nothing more than a five-by-five square opening at the base of the pyramid's north face, are the original granite casing stones. The stones were worked over by ancient stone masons so that they became rounded around the edges, then fitted together irregularly, unlike the other larger pyramids in which the stones were set in neat rows.

In truth, the stonework of the Menkaure pyramid resembles in great detail, the stonework that can be found at Machu Picchu in Peru. It's often left me feeling as if the pyramids occupying the Giza

Plateau are not the work of human hands, but of an intelligence far more advanced than ours could have possibly been five thousand years ago. Aliens don't come to mind here. But the descendants of the lost city of Atlantis most definitely do. It's not as far out a notion as one might think. More than one civilization has been lost to rising tides and changing geographies. Atlantis might very well be only one of them.

Legend has it that when the tomb was opened for the first time in 1830 by Colonel Howard-Vyse of her Majesty's Royal Navy, the sarcophagus of Menkaure was discovered. But, tragically, the ship that was carrying the mummified remains back to mother England sank off the coast of Spain in very deep water, perhaps forever eliminating the opportunity to confirm the true identity of the mummy housed in the tomb.

For centuries the tomb has remained a source of great mystery. While the narrow and low-ceilinged passages that lead down into the roots of the mountainous pyramid will most definitely lead you to a wide, cathedral-ceilinged burial chamber, it is no secret that many more undiscovered passages exist. More than a few of these passages are false and simply lead to dead ends. Other passages are said to lead to chambers that access a great system of aquifers or underground rivers that run beneath the pyramids and connect directly to the Nile, which is no doubt the source of their flow. It is also said by some that these rivers once provided the power-source for the electricity which was generated by the pyramids in ancient times, making the indestructible stone giants not only tombs for the dead Pharaohs, but electrical powerhouses for Egypt's massive ancient civilization. More evidence of the Giza pyramids having been designed by ancient Atlantians? Maybe.

There are, of course, other dangers that exist inside the Third Pyramid, along with false doors, floors, walls and pits. And it's these mortal dangers that no doubt persuaded the Vatican to choose this site to bury the bones of their most beloved Messiah. To say the pyramid posed real threats to those who attempted to seek out its treasures or, in this case, the bones of Christ, is as understated as saying human beings require oxygen to breathe.

I've been here before. So has Dr. Andre Manion. To the desert, I mean. We got as far as working in some of the false chambers located outside the third pyramid. We worked the quote, "mysterious pit," unquote under the cover of darkness and found only passages that led to nowhere, one of which became so gradually narrow as I descended as to be unnoticeable until it was too late, and I found myself hopelessly and relentlessly stuck. If it weren't for the quick thinking of Andre who pulled me out by my booted feet, I might never have made it out alive.

This was all happening during a time when I was not of the most sound mind and soul. Back in New York, my wife had left me for another man and taken my infant daughter with her. Her infidelity had been provoked, or so she claimed in the divorce papers, due to my infidelity with my travels, my writing, my treasure hunting, my search for "the goddamned meaning of my goddamned life." Once my marriage was officially dead and buried, I proceeded to spend the better part of two years bathed in booze, loose women, plane tickets, guiding, and sandhogging. Somehow I managed to write a couple of novels revolving around my adventures as well, although I only have a vague recollection of sitting down long enough to do the actual writing.

We scored nothing on that first dig simply because we were digging in the wrong place. But I did uncover something of value. Rather, something that, according to Andre and his extensive research, might help us uncover the precise space in which the bones of Christ might have been hidden by Vatican experts back in 1978. That item was a mirror that I discovered buried in the pit. It wasn't as if it had been left there by some ancient architect or grave robber. But as if it had been purposely tossed into the pit as recently as '78 by one of the men who buried the bones and who now, wished to make sure the mirror and its direction-finding capabilities were lost to all mankind forever.

I lifted the two pieces of mirror from the rubble in the mysterious pit, not long after Andre had rescued me from sure death inside the third pyramid. For a time I kept the find to myself, until one night, after a particularly good drunk in the bars of Cairo, I came home to my tent and passed out. While one-half of the mirror remained securely stored in my cargo pants pocket, I had stupidly left the other half sitting out on my portable desk where I had been conducting research on it over what was then considered the newest digital research wonder of them all: the Internet. In the morning, the mirror was gone, and although I had no definite proof of who precisely had stolen it, I could only surmise that the guilty party was one of the many Arab diggers we'd hired as cheap labor.

I kept the news of the mirror pieces from Andre for as long as I could. Until the failed dig was long over and he had left Egypt one night totally unannounced and entirely under the cover of darkness, as if he were afraid I would somehow try and stop him or worse, hit him, in my inebriated state of constant rage. In the end, it was his further research that would decide the importance of the mirror, it having been written about in scholarly papyrus texts as old as ancient Egypt itself. The mirror was said to reveal the true location of the last and deepest burial chamber in the Third Pyramid, but only when you fit the mirror into a certain area of stone wall precisely at dawn when the virgin sunlight would shine in through a long, man-made vertical shaft constructed into the rock wall. Andre and I both knew then, and we know now, that under no circumstances would we have a chance of locating the bones of Jesus without that mirror. Now, we not only have a map showing us the home of the bones, we have the mirror which will, God willing, reveal their precise location within the home.

By the time we come upon the pyramids at Giza, it's getting close to dusk. Which suits us just fine.

"Park it here for now, Sameh," I say, far enough in the distance so as not to bring any kind of unwanted attention from Giza security guards or the military police constantly pacing the place with their automatic weapons and sneering faces. I can only surmise that the lights that shine off the pyramids at night will be extinguished soon as a money saving concession to a new government that also shuts off the water and electricity every other day in order to pinch badly needed pounds.

Turning, I face the Land Cruiser's back seat.

"Anya," I say, "think you can manage to mix us up something to eat with the food supplies we have left?"

"So long as Sameh shows me how to use the gas stove," she says, "I'm sure I can manage something."

Then to Andre. "Professor, you and I have some studying up to do, starting with the shroud blueprint."

"I'm dying to see it," he says.

"Let's hope that's not the case," I say.

We all exit the Land Cruiser and go about the work of changing the world.

Forever.

35

Enlarged photos of the shroud CAD blueprint are laid out on top of a map of the Giza pyramids. Also included in the mix is a map of the Mankaure Third Pyramid and its previously known interior chambers. "Previously known," being the key words here.

Manion is using a good old fashioned magnifying glass to examine both the blueprint and the maps, going from one to the other and back again. A long weighted minute ticks by before he straightens up and smiles.

"After all this time, Chase," he says. "After all these years, the answer was right in front of our noses. All we had to do was consult the shroud and all you had to do was find the other half of the mirror. It seems as if God finally wants us to finish the job we started nearly ten years ago."

"Think we can find a way to access these underground chambers, Professor?" I say.

"If we can find the key."

"What key?"

He lifts his head up, sets the magnifying glass down onto the maps.

"A key, a trigger, or a button-like device that will cause a secret door to open in the floor or the wall, or even an empty sarcophagus."

"Secret door," Sameh says like a question. "Sounds like something from out of a movie...*Tomb Raider*."

The professor shrugs, rolls his eyes.

"All the same," he says, "trap doors do exist not only in the third pyramid but in all the great pyramids, and not all of them have been discovered. But the one we must find in the third pyramid will almost certainly lead down to the chambers depicted on the 1978 shroud CAD drawing."

"But how exactly do we find this door much less its key?" Sameh asks.

"It's more or less found us," the professor says, pressing his index finger on the top-most portion of the CAD-rendered tunnel. "You see here, where the tunnel meets the top floor of the now empty tomb?"

We all eye the tip of his index finger where it points to on the map.

"That spot is not a piece of the tomb's floor, but the tomb itself. Or so I believe."

"Menkaure's sarcophagus," I deduce.

"Precisely what I'm thinking," the professor smiles. "Think of it as X marks the spot."

Dinner is consumed quickly and silently. Soon as

it's over, the four of us gather to figure out a plan of attack.

But here's the thing: The plan, as I see it anyway, isn't really much of a plan.

We will head into the chamber after midnight when the lights are extinguished and the guards are asleep. It's true, even guarding one of the most revered ancient wonders of the world can be a real snooze. Sleeping guards or not, gaining access to the third pyramid and the tombs housed deep inside, will require subduing of the guards and, naturally, stealing the keys to an old fashioned padlocked gate (up until recent years, the Giza pyramids weren't locked up at all during off hours!).

"But what about interior security?" I ask. "Hidden cameras, alarms, silent and not so silent?"

We all turn to the fixer.

"So what exactly are we dealing with, Sameh?" I push. "I was under the assumption pyramid security had gone way south now that the radical bandits are in charge of the show."

"On the contrary, the free-for-all days have come to an end at the pyramids," Sameh begins to explain. "Here is the bad news: Since the last time either of your gentlemen led an expedition in Giza, strict security improvements have been made. The entire plateau is surrounded and protected by a twenty-kilometer fence that's equipped with cameras, alarms, and motion detectors. The cameras feed more than twenty-four high-definition television monitors inside a control room which is located at the pyramid tourist entrance. The monitors are observed for suspicious activity twenty-four hours a day, seven days a week. The fence is more than four meters high and cannot possibly be scaled or jumped over without attracting attention since it is dotted with infrared sensors and even more motion detectors."

And here I was thinking all it would take to gain access to the Third Pyramid was to beat up a couple of guards. I feel my heart sink.

"So what's the good news?" Anya poses on behalf of us all.

Sameh's sour face begins to beam with a smile.

"Since the 2010 revolution and the taking over of control by the radical religious element, pyramid security funding has been cut significantly."

"By just how much?" Andre begs.

"All electronic surveillance devices are turned off at midnight in order to save on expenses. Fact is, many strict followers of Islam have even toyed with tearing the pyramids down since they represent the celebration of pagan Gods which is a mortal sin against Allah."

"But this all makes sense," Andre says bitterly. "Since I've been here working at gunpoint, mind you, the government has been shutting down the electricity, and shutting down the water service sometimes on a daily basis. We're in the Middle East and Egypt is plagued by gas shortages for God's sake. Not to mention food shortages, medical supply shortages, even bread shortages. All this, of course, wreaked havoc on the dig."

"A dig that was going nowhere anyway," I add.

"Indeed the case," Andre smiles. "I was running a false dig at gunpoint. But they didn't know it was false. So it was important to give them the impression that the site was legitimate. My life, and in some ways, the life and death of Jesus depended upon it."

Sameh raises a cautious hand.

"But we will still have to contend with the fence and with armed guards who, despite the cutbacks, patrol the area day and night."

"If those men who kidnaped you work for the same boss as those pyramid guards do, Professor," I add, "chances are they might even be expecting us."

"So how exactly shall we plan on getting into the Third Pyramid?" Anya asks.

"That's the major league question isn't it?" I say.

For a moment we listen to the whistle of the wind gently blowing across the desert. Until Andre raises up his right hand, as if to say, *Eureka!* Or *Bingo!* anyway. Slowly, dramatically, raising both his hands up to the stars, he steps out into the desert and begins to recite a not altogether unrecognizable bit of epic poetry, but also a piece that the writer in me recognizes right away.

"*Broken in war, set back by fate,*" he sings, his voice traveling across the desert flats, "*the leaders of the Greek host, as years went by, contrived, with Pallas' help, a horse as big as a mountain. They wove its sides with planks of fir, pretending this was an offering for their safe return. At least, so rumor had it. But inside they packed, in secret, into the hollow sides, the fittest warriors; the belly's cavern, huge as it was, was filled with men in armor.*"

He turns, his smiling teeth reflecting the light of the stars, and comes back to us from out of the desert. Returns triumphantly, I should say.

"Excuse me," Anya says. "But is this going to be another one of your Biblical lectures, Dr. Andre? The ones where you spout off some parable and we're supposed to guess what it is you're getting at? Because frankly I don't think anyone is in the mood and we're not just another group of students who—"

"—No, no, no," he insists, shaking his head hard. "Nothing like that. Actually, the plan I have in mind dates back to the ancient Greeks and *The Fall of Troy*, and we have Virgil to thank for it. After ten brutal years of trying to break through the walls of Troy it finally occurred to them that if they built a giant horse and offered it up as a gift, they might actually get through the gates. But here's the catch: Hiding inside the horse was a big surprise."

"The fittest warriors," I add. "They were hiding inside the horse."

"I see," Anya says. "So we're going to build a horse."

Andre shoots her a look.

"Now I know why we divorced," he says.

"Okay, kids," I break in, "enough with the squabbles. Time's wasting. The professor is making a lot of sense. We don't risk trying to break through the fence and being caught. Instead, we pretend we are actually expected at the Pyramids as archeologists and academics."

"I get it now," Anya offers. "It's not altogether different from how we got into the Turin Cathedral to have an impossible audience with the shroud."

"But this one will be different in one very

important respect," I add.

"And that is?" the college English teacher begs.

"We won't be able to rely on the help of one of Checco's insiders. We're going to have to do some convincing to some potentially nasty bandits all on our own."

Out the corner of my eye, I see Andre fumbling through the many pockets of his bush vest. Eventually, he pulls out what looks to me like a laminated ID card with a neck strap attached to it.

"Credentials," he states proudly. "Archeological credentials. A bit out of date, but I could always feign ignorance. Besides, we try and get through the front gate at half-past midnight, they'll probably be drunk or stoned on hash or both."

"Muslims don't partake," Anya says. "It's against their religion."

"Some don't partake. At least, in public. Emphasis on some."

"So then," I say, my eyes on Sameh, "do you think that by presenting ourselves as an archeological team wishing to work at night to avoid the crowds might work?"

He nods.

"Possibly. But we don't have an appointment and if we aren't on the manifest, there's a good chance they will turn us away and then immediately sic their friends on us. And then there's the possibility of them recognizing Dr. Manion as the archeologist who just got away from their bandit buddies."

"I understand that," I say. "But do you think it's possible that we can at least make it through the gate, if the professor manages to keep a low profile?"

"It's definitely possible."

I lower my head, stare at the LED-lit sandy floor, while I contemplate getting through the front gate without getting myself or anyone else killed.

Then, raising my head, "How much ammo we got left? I think we're gonna need all we can get."

36

An hour later, we are packed up and back inside the Land Cruiser making our way along the desert road on our way towards Giza and the pyramids. The time is eight-thirty on a starry evening. The kind of high-definition clear night that makes you feel like you can reach up and touch the stars.

Over the course of sixty minutes we've revised and tweaked our plan until we have something that just might work. Rather than attempt to hide ourselves under the cover of darkness, we are being very open about our intentions. Which are nothing other than entering into the site of the ancient pyramids as legitimate archeologists and television professionals investigating unknown passages at the bottom of the Third Pyramid crypt. The plot? We are filming a two-part special for the *History Channel* called the *Mysteries of the Menkaure's*

Mini Pyramid.

Before entering into the Giza Plateau, we head back to the same Giza garage that provided us with the Land Cruiser. The tall, bearded, blue-jeans wearing Nisbah is there to greet us while Sameh talks with him about a special, immediate turn-around project. That is, retrofitting the Land Cruiser with some new detailing and some special protection. For these things, we are willing to pay a great deal. Rather, Anya's dead dad is willing to put up the funds.

At the same time, Sameh makes a few calls to some people who specialize in outfitting archeological and television crews.

"If we're going to be presenting ourselves as serious television people," Sameh says, "we'd better look like television people."

"Trojan horse, Sameh," I say. "Make it real."

Two hours later the Land Cruiser is ready to ride once more. A new logo has been added to each door. It's a single pyramid painted in bright red paint. Inscribed inside the pyramid in bright blue letters are the words, *Pharaoh Productions*. The vehicle has not only been outfitted with a bullet-proof windshield and rear window, a special plate made up of quarter inch steel has been welded to the bottom, just in case we should encounter an unexpected improvised explosive device. Stored in the back of the 4X4 are some of the tools of the television trade: cameras both big and small, tripods, lighting and sound equipment, boom stands, and various other props. Placed beside that equipment are all the tools that Andre would require if he were truly embarking on an archeological dig inside the Third Pyramid. An assortment of shovels, Maglites, coal scoops, dust pans, a good old fashioned shaker screen, an electronic transit mapping device, weighing and measuring tools, and even a cordless hammer drill are included in the mix.

Then there are the hidden tools of my trade.

Stored in padlocked metal boxes underneath the equipment, are the four AK47s Sameh provided us with earlier, plus new ammo magazines. Added to the collection are two new RPG rounds for the reusable manual launcher, two more 9mm automatics and accompanying nine-round mags, plus four-night vision goggles, and new two-way radios.

The final touch is our new clothes, courtesy of Nisbah's first cousin who runs an Egyptian cotton export operation on the outskirts of Giza. Each of us has been issued a new khaki safari jacket a piece that bears the Pharaoh Productions logos. For head gear, new *Pharaoh Productions* baseball caps. Stored inside each of our chest pockets are laminated credentials that contain photo IDs and press passes. We also have forged letters from the U.S. Embassy that have been stamped by the Egyptian government stating our intention to film on the pyramid grounds on behalf of the *History Channel*. How Sameh and Nisbah are able to put this Trojan horse operation together in such a short time is both a testament to a race of people who bore the innate organizational talent to build the ancient pyramids and also to the old saying about money talking and bullshit walking.

"What if one of the guards decides to call the *History Channel* in New York to verify our presence?" Anya begs while slipping into her safari jacket. "What if he were to contact the government about our intrusion?"

Sameh's face lights up.

"I've already thought of that. The number printed on the letter will dial not the *History Channel* necessarily but a special friend who will make believe he is a big shot at the *History Channel*. As for the government, we will simply have to take our chances."

A good friend from Florence comes immediately to mind.

"Checco," I say, winking at Sameh.

"Indeed," he nods. "Without Checco and my associate, Nisbah, we could not possibly have put all this together in such a short amount of time. Amazing what can happen when you are blessed by Allah."

"Yes, God be praised," Andre says. "And thank God for my wealthy ex-wife. But what about getting past the front door? If the guards aren't expecting us, they're liable to turn us back no matter whom we ask them to call for verification. That is, unless you plan on shooting our way through which, in my archeological mind, would be entirely counter-productive. Not to mention, really bloody dangerous." He frowns and presses the back of his hand up against the underside of his chin. "I've about had it up to here with playing with guns and bombs."

"Our friend Checco has a made a few calls on our behalf," Sameh assures. "Trust me when I say, the guards will be expecting us."

"But will they believe us?" I say, thumbing the clip release on my 9mm, checking the load, then thumbing the safety on after cocking a fresh round into the chamber.

Our conversation is interrupted by the sound of the newly refurbished Land Cruiser being fired up, as Nisbah proceeds to back it out of the garage and onto the lot.

"Belief in our intentions is not guaranteed," Sameh says. "But I will leave such things up to God."

"And fate," Anya says, turning and heading out through the open overhead garage door.

My beating heart pulsing on my sleeve, I follow.

37

It's going on midnight when we pull up to the main entry for the Giza pyramids. While the colorful pyramid spotlighting has been turned off, the entry facility is still lit up like a Christmas tree with pole and wall-mounted LED security lighting. Sameh pulls up to a security shack and stops the Land Cruiser so that the front grill faces a red and black vertically striped crossing gate.

The guard manning the brightly lit, glass and concrete block-walled shack is wearing the black beret, scarf, and white shirt of a government soldier. He's packing a 9mm automatic on his hip. Mounted to the wall behind him are four AK47s at the ready. Before Sameh can even get the window down, two more soldiers step up to the gate and eyeball us through the windshield.

The window slides open, the guard sneering at

us.

"How can I help you?" he says in deep-throated English.

Sameh reaches into his chest pocket, pulls out his papers, hands them to the guard.

"We're making a documentary for the *History Channel*," he informs, confidence in his tone, the deepest respect in his delivery.

"What is the *History Channel*?" asks the guard, holding the letter in his hand, but his eyes remaining glued to Sameh's.

"It's a cable television channel in the west. Lots of stories about ancient sites from all over the globe. Stories that involve the pyramids are especially popular, for obvious reasons. I'm sure we're not the first film crew and archeological team to make television here."

The soldier stares down at the letter. He reads it, turns it over, sees that nothing is written on the back. Then, holding the letter outside the open window, he waves it at the two guards standing in front of us, and barks something out in Arabic.

"What's he saying?" I ask under my breath.

"Hopefully he's not saying, 'Shoot the lying, spying infidels on the spot,'" Anya says from the back.

"No time for joking," scolds Andre who is seated beside her. He's scrunched down, his *Pharaoh Productions* baseball cap pulled down tightly over his head as if trying to hide or keep a much needed low profile anyway.

Sameh says, "He's asked them if they know anything about a crew arriving at such an odd

220

hour."

The guard on the left suddenly nods, and speaks.

Sameh says, "That guard on the right said he believes someone called not long ago warning of our arrival. But he didn't pay much attention to it."

The soldier in the guard shack shouts something in anger at the soldier on the right.

Sameh translates again: "He said, 'Why wasn't I informed of this? Everything goes through me. Maybe you are drunk.'"

"So they do drink after all," Anya whispers.

"What was your first guess?" Andre says.

My eyes are glued to the soldier in the guard shack now that he's back to staring at the letter. For a brief moment, I think he's about to turn us away or worse: Order his men to open up on us with the AK47s. I slip my hand inside my safari jacket, lightly wrap my hand around the shoulder-holstered pistol grip. But just as I'm about to unholster the piece, the soldier slowly hands the document back to Sameh. At the same time, he triggers a device on a nearby panel that causes the crossing gate to lift up.

The two guards ahead of us back away and make room.

"You may proceed," he says. "But be aware that we are watching your every movement at all times."

"How will we gain access to the Third Pyramid?" Sameh poses to the guard. "Surely it is locked."

"When you arrive you will find that the pyramid entrance is well guarded. I will radio word for them to open the entry gates for you." He grows a sly smile. "Keep in mind that like me, the guards are soldiers of the President's army and are heavily armed."

"Thank you for sharing," Sameh grins. "We will indeed keep that in mind. Salem Allah."

"Allah Salem," the soldier returns. But I can only wonder if he really means it.

The soldier waves his hand in a gesture that resembles him gently slapping someone's behind.

"You may proceed," he says.

Sameh shifts the Land Cruiser into first, gently taps the gas, pulls forward.

The Trojan Horse worked.

We're in. But for how long?

38

We follow the cobbled road on its gently sloping uphill climb through the northern edge of the Giza Plateau. In the desert darkness, the three pyramids loom over us not like huge, triangular piles of seventy-ton blocks of solid Aswan limestone, but instead, sheer mountains that dominate the landscape. Hooking a right, Sameh drives off-road and heads across the flat desert past some rectangular ruins of what was once a temple and beside it, a settlement constructed for the Egyptian workers who were conscripted to build the great pyramids. Moments later we arrive at Mankaure's tomb.

As promised, there are two guards watching over the pyramid's entrance.

They occupy a piece of ground about ten feet in front of the tomb door. It's protected by a small wall-less hut constructed of a wood roof supported by four metal poles. Their white and black uniforms are illuminated in the dull white light that oozes from a single exposed light bulb that hangs overhead. We pull up to their hut and exit the vehicle.

Sameh greets the two guards with the peace and love of Allah. They greet him back, while at the same time, keeping an ever ready hand on the automatic assault rifles which are strapped to their shoulders.

"You are the TV," says the first man like a question. He's not tall or short, but he bears a thick black mustache which he is constantly grooming with the thumb and forefinger on his free, left hand.

"You should be expecting us," states Sameh.

Mustached man shoots a glance over at his taller, thinner, clean-shaven partner. Clean Shaven Partner nods, winks.

I don't like the wink. It sends a chill up and down my backbone.

"You may unload your gear," says Mustached Man. Then, to his partner. "Help them."

Without a word, Clean Shaven Partner makes his way to the Land Cruiser's tailgate.

Anya shuffles over to me.

"I don't like this," she whispers. "Something's not right."

"Just stay close to me," I insist, speaking under my breath. "I agree. I'm not getting the warm and fuzzies from these guys either. But then we have no choice but to play the game."

Sameh opens the tailgate while Andre assists in

unpacking some of the gear. He lifts a camera onto his shoulder while Anya grabs some of the sound equipment, and I grab hold of the cordless hammer drill. Meanwhile, Sameh grabs two of the Maglites, handing one to me.

"I suggest we find out precisely what we're dealing with inside," barks Andre, "before we lug the rest of the equipment all the way down into the tomb."

Knowing that hidden directly below the archeology and camera equipment is our arsenal of weapons, I cannot agree more.

"Good idea," I say, closing the hatchback. Then, "Gentlemen and lady," I say, taking the lead position, "the body of Christ Almighty is among us."

39

The interior lighting inside the pyramid's tight opening is dim and sparse, but at least it is operational. It's a straight shot down a rectangular tunnel so narrow and cramped that we are forced to crouch while maintaining our balance on the steep, thirty-five-degree downward decent. We hold to banisters mounted to the stone walls with our free hands while lugging the equipment with the others. Attached to the floor are wood boards that act as ladder rungs to keep us from sliding down into the tombs on our backsides.

Keeping a close watch on our tail are the two guards. I never counted on them entering into the pyramid along with us, and I know the others didn't either. If the rest of my team is thinking like me, they know that sooner or later, the guards will have to be dealt with. Just how we're going to deal with them, I haven't the slightest clue. Of course, I could just shoot them. But that would be murder. Murder is not my strong suit. Chase the kind.

We make it onto the first landing, which also accesses a small storage area that once housed treasures that Menkaure would carry with him into eternity and beyond. Golden chariots, royal beds (one for every night of the week so that the evil Gods would never know precisely where he was sleeping on any given ancient evening), mummified remains of favorite pets, plus chairs, toys, bows and arrows, food, even solid gold statues of royal guards whose job it would be to guard the tomb against intruders. Now the treasure is all gone, looted not long after the tomb was first sealed thousands of years ago, the loot no doubt taking up precious space in a wealthy private collector's home museum.

Located at the end of the landing is another narrow tunnel that runs almost the identical length of the first one. Leading the way, I don't hesitate to begin the climb down towards what I know will be Mankaure's tomb which still houses his empty sarcophagus. If the professor's academic opinion is correct, the sarcophagus contains a secret door that will provide entry into an unknown series of antechambers and crypts.

I come to the bottom of the tunnel, step onto the landing.

It's at this point, the electric light, such as it is, ends, and what lies ahead is draped within a blackness so thick and so seemingly eternal, it makes my throat constrict and my mouth go dry. Unlike the air outside, the atmosphere inside the room is cool, moist, smells of must and, dare I say it, death. Directly before me is a large, square arch created from the same perfectly carved limestone as the walls that surround it, the joints in between the stones so narrow, so perfect, I defy anyone to stick a fingernail into it without getting it stuck.

I flick on the Maglite.

"Careful, old boy," Andre warns from behind. "Little booby traps can pop out at us from anywhere at any time."

"In this tourist trap?" I say, feigning my tough guy stance.

"Didn't say anything about traps set by the ancients. I'm thinking more along the lines of traps set by our new radical, extremist Muslim friends."

"Hey you, infidel," barks one of the attending guards, "you keep your mouth shut about the faith of Allah. I would be happy to shoot you in the back."

I make out the sound of Anya chuckling under her breath.

"Boys will be boys," she whispers.

"Please," Sameh scolds, as though his nerves are getting to him the closer we all come to entering into the cold, darkened chamber. "Focus on the task ahead."

Thumbing the latex-covered black button on the Maglite, I shine its powerful round beam of white light into the burial chamber.

It's then I see the face of a man staring back at me.

40

I know this face.

I know this man.

Because I shot him in the leg only this morning out in the desert. He is the man whom I first saw in the Kings Hotel Bar. The man who followed me to Amun's antique shop in the bazaar. The wealthy oil man responsible for kidnapping Andre.

More flashlights ignite in both directions.

For a brief second or two I am blinded. The same few seconds I use to draw my 9mm from my shoulder holster, thumb back the trigger, aim the barrel for the mustached man's face.

"If you breathe," I say, "I will send you straight to hell."

From behind me comes the sound of small arms being cocked. Then, stepping from out of the dark chamber and into the light, two bandits dressed in long robes.

"Sameh," I say, shooting a glance over my shoulder at him. He too has drawn his weapon and has it aimed at the bandits. He's also holding the bright beam of Maglite on them, pointing it at their eyes, as if trying to blind them.

I glance over my other shoulder.

Both Andre and Anya too have weapons drawn. God bless them. They are waving the weapons not at the bandits protecting the injured Mustached Man, but at the guards who accompanied us down here. The same guards who now also have their weapons aimed directly for our brain pans.

"You are surrounded, Chase Baker," says Mustached Man, wincing from the pain in his wounded leg. "You have no choice but to put down your weapons."

"You look pale," I say, holding my aim directly for the thin space between his eyes. "That leg must really smart."

"You leave me with little choice but to shoot you, right here, down inside this cold, cold crypt."

"You won't kill us. You want the bones. So long as we know where the bones are and you don't, you're not going to shoot us. Besides, your men take a shot at us, you are the first to die. Be a shame to spatter your brains all over this ancient wonder of the world."

He attempts a smile, but he's in so much pain I can see the hurt in his gray teeth.

"I didn't say I would kill you," he grins. "I said I would shoot you. But I will keep you alive long enough to retrieve the information I need in order to locate the bones."

"He wants to torture us," Sameh says, steadily holding both his gun and the Maglite on the bandits.

"Thanks for the translation," I say.

"Chase," Anya says. "I've never killed anyone before."

"Might be a good time to start," Andre says.

"Mexican stand-off," I say, glancing down at the small puddle of blood that's collecting around the Mustached Man's left foot. Then, staring into his dark eyes, "We're not giving up our weapons. So what do you plan on doing now? You gonna bleed on us?"

He doesn't answer me. Instead he barks something in Arabic which results in he and his robed bandits slowly back-stepping into the darkness.

"Keep a bead on them, Sameh," I bark. "And the light."

We follow them into the dark chamber.

Behind me, I listen to the footsteps of Anya and Andre, and the guards close on our heels.

"Something's got to give, Chase," Sameh says.

That's when it comes to me. Shifting my flashlight to the right, I spot Menkaure's empty sarcophagus. A vault that was carved out of solid granite. It's positioned up against the far wall.

"Anya," I say, a little under my breath. "I need you to listen to me."

"I'm listening."

"I want you to go to the crypt and lie down inside it. Andre will cover you."

"It's a goddamned coffin, Chase."

"Do it now," I insist.

I watch Mustached Man's ever shifting eyes as she side steps to the sarcophagus, all the time, keeping her weapon poised on the two pyramid guards. When she places one foot into the crypt, I pull the Maglite away so that she becomes completely hidden in darkness.

I shift the light so that it shines directly into Mustached Man's face. Droplets of sweat are dripping off his forehead, into his bloodshot eyes, making them sting. Or so I imagine.

"Sameh, Andre," I say, under my breath. "Follow my lead. I'll take out the flashlights. You take out the bandits."

Those pain-filled eyes on Mustached Man go wide like he knows precisely what's coming. And he does.

"Shoot them!" he barks, as my finger comes down on the trigger and the burial chamber goes black.

41

The tomb explodes in gunfire and bright, instantaneous gunpowder flashes.

I take out the flashlight, drop onto my right side, pour all nine rounds into Mustached Man and his bandits. The show only takes a few seconds from start to finish. When it's over, I shine the Maglite behind me. I see that the two guards are dead, what's left of their heads spread all over the stone floor like raspberry jam.

Sameh in still lying on the floor, his baseball cap having fallen off.

Andre is lying beside him.

I call out to them. But no one makes a move or a sound.

Lifting myself onto my knees, I shoot a look at Mustached Man and the bandits. He is lying on his back, his mouth and eyes wide open. He's more dead than the stone that surrounds him. As I attempt to stand, I see movement coming from one of his bandits. I see his AK being raised until I'm staring into all eternity.

The shot rings out.

I take a quick step back. I don't know if I've been hit or not.

But then I see the bandit's head drop down onto the floor. It sounds like a melon tossed against the stone. I turn toward the crypt and see Anya standing inside it. She's got her pistol gripped in both her hands, her arms still extended and aimed for the now dead bandit, a slight trickle of smoke rising from out of the barrel.

"You're pretty good with that thing," I say, my voice echoing inside the hollow stone chamber.

My words break her out of her spell.

"Andre!" she shouts.

Her ex-husband is gathering himself up off the floor. Slowly. The look on his face is not pain, but disgust. Sickness for the grisly task he had no choice but to perform.

"I am a scientist," he says, tossing the pistol. "Not a killer."

"It's over now," I say as if offering a condolence. Then, "Sameh. Are you okay?"

He's still lying on his side, his back to me, his bare head pointing to the chamber entrance.

"Sameh," I repeat going to him, dropping down onto my knees, rolling him over.

That's when I see the single hole in his forehead, the bullet having exited out the top of his head. A wound that killed him instantly.

I feel my heart go south, as if it's suddenly turned to limestone.

"My friend," I exhale, feeling the tears fill my eyes.

"What do you want to do?" Andre whispers. "There will be more guards coming for us."

I take a moment to breathe. To listen to my aching heart. To say goodbye to Sameh. But time to grieve is not time we can afford. My mind swims with memories of nighttime ambushes in both the sands of Iraq and the rocky valleys of Afghanistan, and the gurgling sounds my friends made just before they died from bullets to the neck or face. You want to lay down your weapon, curl up, and weep on the spot. But you can't. You reach out, close their eyelids, say a silent—but oh so brief—prayer that you hope will be heard by God if he exists. Then you slap a new mag into your M4, cover your tear-filled eyes with night vision goggles, lift yourself up from off the ground and resume the fight. Life is fleeting in times of war. Death is even more so.

I stand, and change out the clip on my gun.

My eyes on Andre and Anya, I say, "The mortal remains of the Lord is resting somewhere inside this pyramid. We must do what we came here to do."

Andre raises a smile that is anything but happy. But Anya does something different. She comes to me, gently kisses me on the cheek.

"I was wrong," she says. "You do care about us. You saved our lives."

"You saved mine. Twice. Makes us more than even."

She kisses me again, then turns, makes her way back over to the empty sarcophagus.

42

Before we begin our search down under, I make my way back to the pyramid's entry, head back out to the Land Cruiser. Opening the tailgate, I locate the RPG launcher and slide in a round. From there I carry the weapon, plus a roll of duct tape and some monofilament fishing line with me back inside the small entry. Positioning the RPG up against the wall and against the underside of the exposed metal electrical conduit, I proceed to duct tape the RPG to the metal tubing.

When that's done, I tie more of the filament line to the trigger mechanism, run it around the trigger guard and all the way to the steel-barred gate. Closing the gate and padlocking it, I then make the filament line taut and tie it off onto the gate's middle bar. I know that it's only matter of minutes until a new team of guards make their way back up here. When they do, they are in for quite the surprise.

Turning and crouching, I make my way back down into the chamber and re-join the others. Andre and Anya are already scouring the sarcophagus for any secrets it might reveal, using their Maglites to illuminate their work.

"How many times over the centuries has this tomb been examined and re-examined?" I say, adding my own beam of Maglite to the effort.

"Countless times," Andre says. He's kneeling inside the sarcophagus, literally feeling the smooth, carved, stone interior with his fingertips. "But, other than the team assembled by the Vatican back in 1978, it's quite possible I am the first man or woman to be examining it for a secret door or opening. In some ways, that makes this the first time Mankaure's eternal resting place has ever truly been researched."

"Exactly what are you looking for, Andre?" Anya asks.

"A small patch or area that is inconsistent with the others. It might be a rough patch of stone, or the tiniest of protrusions or indentations that, if you weren't looking for it, you might never know was there."

"It's all so smooth," I say.

"That's the deceiving part," Andre says, slowly moving his fingertips over the rock. "You wouldn't think to look for anything here other than what it appears to be. A sarcophagus carved in granite and that's all."

Anya and I stand in silence while we watch him

work.

Until his fingers suddenly stop.

"That's it," he says. "That has got to be it."

"What is it?" Anya says, pointing her light to a spot in which his index finger has stopped moving.

I feel my heartbeat pick up. I might be a writer now, but the sandhog in me has never gone away.

"This is a trigger for a counterweight," Andre says. Then, turning his head to me over his shoulder. "Chase, would you happen to have a coin?"

I dig into my pocket, pull out a single Egyptian pound, hand it to Andre. He takes the coin and gently slips it into a slot that I would never have located with my naked eye. Turing the coin counter-clock-wise, he leans back.

"Get back everyone. I'm not sure what's going to happen. Watch for something to drop from the ceiling or the walls. A weight of some kind or even a heavy block."

I hear a distinct click that echoes inside the chamber. Quickly Andre takes to his feet, jumps out of the tomb. Together, the three of us eye the bottom of the tomb as it begins to tremble. The trembling is accompanied by a rock grinding on rock sound as the bottom of the tomb begins to slowly drop down revealing an open space beneath it. At the same time, behind us, a small portion of the chamber's ceiling opens up. It begins to rain sand and gravel down onto the floor. The counterweight is revealed.

"My God," Anya states, her wide eyes glued to the moving rock.

"Exactly," I say.

The entire right side of the tomb's bottom slab then drops and stops.

"Look," Andre announces. "It's a ramp."

"For climbing down inside," I add, stating the obvious.

I shine the light into the newly formed opening. It's a tunnel not unlike the ones we've already descended into the tomb, only narrower. Tighter. Far shorter, too.

"Who's going first?" Anya asks.

"I'll do it," Andre says.

I take hold of his arm.

"Not a chance, Professor," I say. "There's some kind of booby trap waiting for us down there, better that I deal with it. You're the scientist. I'm the hired muscle."

"You put it that way, Chase old man," he smiles. "Be my guest."

"Easy, Renaissance Man," Anya interjects. "Bravery will get you good and killed."

"So will stupidity," I say.

Setting my posterior onto the sarcophagus wall, I swing my booted feet over the side and set them down onto the angled stone.

"Watch my back," I say.

Pointing the Maglite into the ancient unknown, I enter into the tunnel.

43

Because of the angle and the smooth flatness of the stone, I am forced to descend the ten foot long ramp and the cramped, twenty-plus feet of descending tunnel it accesses from down on my ass until I come to a stone floor. That's when I turn and look back up at two faces looking down upon me.

"Anya," I say. "Send down a rope, and the hammer drill."

She does it, sliding both items down the ramp.

Forced to crawl back up the tunnel, I take hold of the cordless hammer drill with one hand, grab hold of the rope with the other. Because this half ton of perfectly engineered stone ramp operates like a well-balanced see-saw, I can easily move it up and down with only my pinky finger if I so choose. It means that if the guards invade the tomb, I can easily seal the entry back up.

The equipment in hand, I once more make my way back down the tunnel and prepare myself for entering into the unknown chamber. But first things first. The place is pitch dark. Setting the tools down, I pull the Maglite from my pant waist, shine the bright light on the chamber's interior, careful to look for anything that might cause my immediate injury and/or death.

I find it right away.

Shining the light down at me feet, I can see that the area of stone I am walking on can't be more than three feet wide. If I were to take another step, I would drop immediately into a pit. I shine the light into the pit, poke my head over the edge. I can't see bottom so much as something that appears to be in motion and at the same time reflects the light. Like an underground stream or river. Like I've already mentioned, I've heard legends of the pyramids being constructed over underground aquifers, but I've never actually seen evidence of them. Until now. It also explains how the 1978 Vatican team might have gained access to the secret crypt. Not through the Mankaure sarcophagus's secret trap door, in which they would have upset the counter-weight, but instead by having entered through the pit that accesses the underground river. All that would have been required of them was to scale the pit's stone walls like an expert rock climber scaling a cliff.

As far as I can tell, the room is perfectly circular; almost tube-like. There's a solid stone ceiling that's maybe ten feet overhead. The walls are also solid, other than a small, square-shaped opening located directly across the pit from me. I can only assume this is the narrow shaft designed thousands of years ago to capture the sun as it rises during the dawn. If that's the case, there must be a place located on the circular wall directly opposite it which will accept the ancient mirror I presently have stored in my trouser pocket along with the cross I stole off the Vatican soldier back in Florence. Shining the light on the portion of wall to my left, I locate the precise section of indented wall. Pulling the mirror from my pocket, I fit one piece into the space, and then set the second broken piece into the space beside it. It fits together like two missing puzzle pieces, and as exactly and tightly as the blocks in the Third Pyramid's limestone walls.

My heart pounds.

"Professor," I yell up into the tunnel. "This is it. This is the crypt. Down here."

"How do you know?" he shouts.

I tell him about the sun shaft, the mirror, the indented space on the wall.

"I'm coming down," he says.

A minute and a half later, he and Anya are standing beside me.

"This is incredible," she says, her wide eyes gazing upon the secret room. "We're the first modern humans to set our eyes on this place."

"Not really," I say. "A group of Vatican soldiers stood here only thirty-five years ago."

The truth I speak of does nothing to deflate her sense of wonder.

Andre is already consumed with reading the hieroglyphs on the walls.

"Look," he says with all the enthusiasm of a small child. "This image here. The fertility image." He points to a male phallus that is erect and discharging semen in a long steady flow. Inscribed beside it is a replica of a sperm cell. "See what's happening here? This is a microscopic image of a basic sperm cell. Yet the first recorded microscopic sighting of sperm wasn't documented until the age of Galileo in the early sixteen hundreds."

"So what's that prove?" I ask.

"That the ancient Egyptians, including Mankaure, may have been assisted by beings from another world over three to five thousand years ago."

"Aliens," I joke. "Thought you were a scientist, Professor?"

He gives me a look.

"How would you explain this, Chase?"

Anya runs her hands along the inscribed image.

"He's right, Chase. How could the ancient Egyptians know what a sperm cell looks like much less devise the engineering to make this pyramid? To make these secret shafts? The engineering is perfect even by today's standards."

"Perhaps the pyramids were designed by an advanced ancient civilization which has since disappeared," I suggest. "Atlantians, maybe. It would also explain the construction of the Mayan pyramids, and Macchu Picchu."

"And look at this," Andre goes on. He's reading the glyphs that inscribe the wrap-around wall with the same ease that I would apply in reading a newspaper. "See this here. It's the sun god Ra, looming over the head of Menkaure's body as Anubis the jackal prepares his body for mummification." His finger not on Anubis or Ra, but on a figure above them ... a figure in the sky. "Notice the ovular-like shape, and how it's spitting out something that looks like fire from beneath it."

I take a good look, going so far as to shine my light on it.

"I guess that could be a spaceship, Professor," I say, not without giggle. "Maybe it's the heavens opening up for the newly dead Pharaoh. Or maybe it's just some silly, artsy, scribble-work."

"Maybe," Andre admits, taking a step or two back, but careful not to go over the edge. "One thing is for certain. That sarcophagus upstairs wasn't intended as the final resting place of Menkaure. The ancient Egyptians wished for him to be buried right here. Down inside this secret crypt."

"Not so secret crypt," I say. "Remember, the Vatican knows all about it."

He shakes his head.

"How they discovered it and were able to keep it a secret for three, almost four decades is mind boggling to me."

"I think there's quite a bit the Vatican knows about ancient civilizations. Especially about the things that could threaten to destroy their two-thousand-year reign as the most popular religion on earth."

Another glance at my watch.

"How long until the dawn?" Andre says.

"Maybe another fifteen minutes."

"You think we have that kind of time?" Anya

asks.

"Not sure we've got much of a choice but to wait it out," I say. "I did my best to make sure whoever comes our way will, at the very least, be slowed down."

"I don't want to know what you've done, Ren Man," Anya says.

I might enjoy a good laugh over her comment if the explosion from the tripped RPG doesn't rock the Third Pyramid.

44

"Hell was that?" Andre, wide-eyed, biting down on his bottom lip.

"Welcoming party I left for the guards up at the tomb entrance."

"They're gonna find us, kill us, and take the bones, take over the world," Anya laments. Her face has turned pale from anxiety.

"Not if they don't know how to find us," I reassure her. But it's like spitting in the ocean.

I enter back into the tunnel, climb back up to the ramp and, gripping its edge with my right hand, push it back into place. The fit is so precise, so perfectly designed, it actually seals itself together. I have no doubt that from up inside the burial chamber, the empty tomb will appear to be just that … an empty tomb.

But I also know that, eventually, the bandits will

uncover the secret of the tomb and uncover the secret chamber. After all, the sand that supported the counterweight is there on the chamber floor as evidence. Without a proper counterweight, all it will take is for someone to simply push down on the sarcophagus floor to make it fly back open.

Once more joining the others, I check my watch.

"We don't have a lot of time," I say. "Dawn should be here within a minute."

With all eyes focused on the shaft opening located directly across the open pit, we wait.

"Kill the flashlights," I say. "And press your backs up against the wall. As tightly as you can. You never know what can happen when the sun hits the mirror."

"This is it, Chase," Andre says, that same boy-like excitement in his voice. "The moment I've been waiting for, for more years than I care to count."

I feel a set of fingers slipping themselves into the palm of my hand.

Anya.

I take her hand, hold it tightly. Then, something miraculous happens. The long, narrow, stone shaft begins to fill with light like a test tube filling with blood. Not a bright light at first, but a faint glow. It's as if the narrow shaft were an old fashioned light bulb filament beginning to get its glow on. The red/orange light quickly begins to intensify however, becoming brighter and brighter until the now bright white light shoots out from the shaft like a laser beam from a ray gun. The concentrated narrow beam then shoots across the room and collides with the mirror embedded into the stone wall beside us, causing yet another bright beam to bounce off of it at a forty-five degree angle to reveal the precise location of the secret chamber.

The chamber that will more than likely contain the mortal remains of Jesus.

We waste no time.

Andre makes his way carefully past Anya and me and goes to the location of the chamber. Like he did earlier with the tomb, he uses his fingers to feel along the wall.

He turns.

"Chase," he says. "The hammer drill."

Just like old times…The sandhog is about to get dirty again…

I gather up the cordless tool outside the entry to the tunnel, bring it to Andre. At his direction, I press the chisel end in the very spot indicated by his extended index finger, and let her rip. It doesn't take a whole lot of effort for the five-by-five foot piece of false stone-and-mortar wall to crumble, revealing a small crypt.

"The wall must have been carefully reconstructed by the Vatican team in '78," Andre explains. "I would have missed it entirely if not for the mirror."

He forces his way in, shining the flashlight inside the cramped space.

"What do you see?" shouts Anya from behind me.

I poke my head inside, shine the Maglite onto the floor.

"There, Professor," I say. "On the floor. In the

very back."

"I see it," he says. "Get in here, Chase."

Crouching, I shove my way inside. The closer I come to the box I can see that it's been wrapped in a shroud made of cloth. In the decades since it's been placed here, the shroud has become ratty and moth-eaten. Andre drops to his knees, removes the cloth to reveal a red metal strongbox, not unlike the kind of security deposit box you might find inside a bank vault in Switzerland. Wrapped around the box's length and width is a section of chain that's been padlocked. The chain fits so tightly to the locked strongbox, I can't even get a finger under it.

"We need something to break the chain," Andre says.

"I could put a bullet into the padlock. But even then, we're not getting into that box without the help of a pro."

Then, a noise. The sound of a rock-on-rock seal breaking. Followed by the heavy bang and thud.

"The ramp's been lowered," Anya says.

"No time for messing with the padlock," I insist. "Andre, we have to go."

"Where to?" he says, standing.

"Good question," I say, stuffing the thin end of the Maglite into my pant waist.

There's nothing in front of us other than solid wall. Already I can make out the heavy, jackbooted footsteps from the bandits descending the stone, trap-door ramp. I look down, make out the faint sound of running water.

"There," I say. "We go there."

"How?" Anya says.

The guards are shouting. Shouting at us to stop. Automatic weapons being cocked.

"We jump," I say.

45

We stand at the edge of the pit.

"You two go first," I say, pulling my weapon, firing three rounds up into the ramp tunnel. "I'll hold them back."

Andre is holding the box tightly in his arms as if it's a live child and not the bones of a man dead two-thousand years. A most important man. The most important man to have ever lived.

Shots are fired from the tunnel, the rounds ricocheting and sparking off the stone wall opposite us. More screaming. More stomping of footsteps. I return the fire.

"We have to do this, Professor. Do it now. Or we're dead anyway!"

While keeping my gun poised on the bandits, I glance over my shoulder to see Andre set the box onto the stone floor.

"You take the box, Chase," he says. "I'll take my wife."

Despite this rapidly closing door, I can't help but feel a twinge of sadness and even envy, as Anya and her ex-husband take hold of one another's hands and go over the edge. But I don't have time for sentiment as I empty the remainder of the clip into the charging guards and, re-holstering the weapon, pick up the box, cradle it tightly in my arms.

As several shots whizz past my head and careen off the wall opposite me, I stare down into a watery pit, the darkness of which is now broken by two separate white Maglites. I have no idea if the man and the woman who belong to those Maglites are dead or still alive. But then what choice do I have but to jump?

Stepping off the edge, Jesus and I fall.

46

I land inside a deep pool of cold water. Shockingly cold. Water, no doubt, that comes directly from a Nile feeder. With the box still gripped firmly in my arms, I find myself spinning. Round and round like a vinyl record on an old-fashioned turntable. I yell out for Anya and Andre, silently praying to whatever God is up there that they landed safely.

When the word "Here!" echoes off the cave walls, I breathe a sigh of relief. But the relief is short-lived. The spinning is becoming more rapid, more forceful. I am beginning to feel myself being sucked into a whirlpool.

"Professor! Anya!" I call. "You okay?"

"Yes, we're okay," he responds.

"Okay," Anya follows.

"Listen carefully," I go on. "We are going to be sucked under. I can only assume that there is a blow hole of some sort and that we will be spit out of it. Don't fight it. Just hold your breath and hang on. Do you understand?"

"Yes, we understand!" Andre assures.

I manage to catch a quick glimpse of them as they near the center of the whirlpool. They are gripped in one another's arms, their mouths open, barely perched above the foamy water's surface like a starlings begging for food. I try and keep a wide eye on them, until just like that, they disappear beneath the water's surface.

Then it's my turn.

I too have something held tightly in my arms. But it's not a loved one exactly. What is wrapped in my arms are none other than the bones of Jesus. The surreal color of the situation boggles even my mind. I am about to be sucked under this raging vortex of violently spinning underground river water hundreds of feet beneath an ancient pyramid and wrapped inside my arms is the body of Christ. Literally.

I enter into the center, spinning so fast I can almost feel my brain pressing against my skull. And then, as if it's God's will, I am sucked under.

47

How does one describe being pulled rapidly through a smooth tube of rock so fast you can barely keep your mouth shut and your arms from opening and losing the one treasure that is more important than anything you have ever touched. Maybe even more important than your own child.

You don't try and describe it. You just ride the wave, as they say, and wait for it to end. *Hope* for it to end. And when it does, you are literally spit out the side of stone cliff face that empties one hundred or more feet below into the swift moving Nile River.

I fall through the air and hit the water with a painful burning slap to my right side. But at least I'm alive to feel the pain. The pull of the current is swift in the springtime, and I'm having almost as much trouble keeping my head above water as I did inside the whirlpool. The box still wrapped in my arms, I am searching frantically for Anya and Andre. But I can't seem to locate them.

I travel another twenty or thirty feet. Or is it another one hundred feet? The river is moving so fast it's hard to tell just how much distance I'm covering at any given time. But soon enough the river's current slows. The water begins to pool into a kind of placid lake, the bright morning sunshine gleaming off its smooth and almost serene surface. Floating along, bobbing in the slight wake, I gaze over my right shoulder to see Anya kneeling on a sandy riverbank. She's kneeling over a prone Andre. My heart begins to slide south, and I sense what's happened even before I begin to paddle, one-armed, over to the shore.

When I finally make it, I can hear the gentle cries and sniffles of a distraught woman. Setting the box down onto the sand, I go to her.

"He hit his head on a rock as we were pulled down river," she says. "He hit his head and never woke up. It was all I could do to pull him ashore."

Gazing down at Andre, I can easily make out the egg-shaped portion on his forehead directly above the right eye that's been cracked open. A steady stream of blood runs down from it. I would check his pulse just to make sure he is dead, but I've seen way too many dead men in my life to know one when I see one. And Dr. Andre Manion's soul has most definitely exited this world.

I set my hand on Anya's shoulder.

She wipes her eyes with the back of her hands and stands.

"What will we do now?" she says, turning to me.

In the distance, the skyline of Cairo looms large over the troubled, congested city. To our left, the Giza plateau and the pyramids look as solid and majestic in the sunshine as they will continue to look for another five thousand years. Maybe twenty thousand years. Long after human beings have killed themselves off.

"We can't go back there," I say. "It's far too hot."

"Where will we go then, Chase?" She's crying, wiping away her tears as she speaks.

Out on the river now, a felucca is slowly making its way downriver, which in Egypt means that it is flowing in a northerly direction. We'll go north to Alexandria, I say. From there we'll grab a boat across the Mediterranean Sea since we can't very well baggage-check the bones of Christ on commercial airliner. We'll go north to the boot heel of Italy and hop a train to Florence. From there we will enlist the help of Checco. He'll know how to handle the bones from there.

We both find our eyes drifting down at the padlocked box.

"When are we going to open it?"

"Even if we could open it, I wouldn't do it here. Not until we are far away from this danger zone."

She looks up into a brilliant blue sky.

"They could be watching us right now," she says. "The Egyptian government. Even the Vatican. The Israeli Antiquities Authority. Satellites are all powerful."

"God is more powerful," I say. "And he's telling

me to not even think about opening the box until we are far away from here."

"Are you becoming a believer amidst all this death?" she whispers, the words sounding like they're tearing themselves from the back of her throat.

"I hold in my hands the body of Jesus," I say. Then, with my eyes on Andre. "I hope that Jesus was worth saving."

She steals another look at her former husband and quietly weeps. But then, as if determined not to dwell on her past, both immediate and long ago, she sucks in a breath and stops crying.

"How can anyone not believe at a time like this?" she says.

"Yes," I say. "How can I not believe?"

Raising up my right arm, I wave at the felucca. After a moment or two, the pilot catches sight of me, and knowing he's just found himself a fare, he begins sailing for shore.

The time to get the hell out of Egypt has arrived.

48

My smartphone is still operable. I use it to call Checco, who arranges for us to be picked up by a fishing vessel off the Alexandria coast. The boat will be waiting for us so that we don't have to waste time hiding out in the busy and bandit-filled port. But before all that, we find a quiet place along the river. A place where the river runs deep and still. A place where the river is bordered by riverbanks of sand dunes, palm and olive trees, and open sky. It's there we bury Andre "at sea," slipping his mortal remains over the side.

With my hand pressed against the box of bones, I say a small prayer for the man I barely knew, but for whom I was a sandhog years ago when he first went after the remains of Jesus. I remember thinking how absurd the mission was, but then, I wasn't entirely convinced of its absurdity either.

When our digs came up with nothing other than an ancient mirror that I took for my own and I began to drink myself over a marriage gone horribly wrong back in New York, the dig in the desert came to an end, and Andre ran out.

But I can't say I ever held his actions against him.

Even now as I watch his prone body sink beneath the river's surface, his face disappearing into a clear watery obscurity, I can't say I harbor any anger for him. I can only thank him for having come back into my life, and for him to have known the joy, however briefly, of having his theories about the Shroud of Turin, the Third Pyramid at Giza, and the present day location of the bones of Christ, proven true.

"Rest in peace, Professor," I whisper, while Anya looks on tight-lipped, refusing to shed any more tears. "You now belong to the history you so loved."

With a brisk wind behind us, we rode the river for as far as the felucca would take us. From the riverbank, we hiked it up to the highway where we were able to hail down a truck driver who had no problem allowing us to hitch a ride in the back along with a few crates of live chickens. In the end, we arrived in Alexandria some four hours later as the sun was setting on the western horizon.

The commercial fishing boat Checco promised was waiting at the quay. It was an old, rusty boat, filled with maybe a half dozen fisherman who spoke no English and who sported full beards, leathery skin, and barrel chests. We tried to stay out of their way as much as possible and with the captain having given over his quarters to us, it wasn't that difficult. Anya slept most of the way while trying to recover not from the adventure in the desert, so much as digesting the sudden death of her ex-husband. I gave her as much space as I possibly could manage aboard a vessel that wasn't much larger than your average school bus.

Arriving in Calabria, we took the high-speed train north through Rome all the way to Florence. We went straight to my apartment on the Via Guelfa which by then had been cleared and cleaned of all traces of the Vatican soldier who lie bleeding on the floor after I shot him in the leg and relieved him of his cross.

Which brings us to the present ...

Now, on the big wood table in the brick and wood-beamed dining room off the kitchen, sits the red strongbox. Locked and padlocked, as if to expose its contents without proper ceremony will cast a plague on the earth. Behind it is a window that looks out onto the back terrace and the grape arbor, the bright afternoon sun shining down on it, almost peacefully. With the French window panes wide open, I can feel the spring breeze and smell the sweet air.

"How do you plan on getting it open?" Anya asks. "Shouldn't we call Checco? Or Detective Cipriani?"

"We need to let them know we're back," I agree. "But not yet. Right now I prefer that no one knows we're here."

"Do you think we've been followed?"

"I don't know. It's possible."

"Back to my original question. How are we going to get the box open?"

"I'll take care of that," says the man who steps out of the kitchen and into the dining room.

"Guess that answers the question about being followed," I say.

The man smiles. The smile beneath his closely cropped salt and pepper beard is a pleasant one. If he wasn't holding a gun on me right now, I just might smile back. But I'm not in a smiling mood as a man whom I considered a friend is now proving that friendship doesn't mean shit when it comes to greed.

"Sorry I have to do this, Chase," says Detective Cipriani, "but business is business." Then, gazing quickly over his left shoulder. "Boys!"

Out from the kitchen come two men. Both dark-haired, clean-shaven and dressed entirely in black. Both look big enough to bench press the Duomo. Former cops maybe. Or maybe cops in real-time, moonlighting for their corrupt day boss.

Anya steps up beside me. Takes hold of my arm.

"It's okay, Anya," I say, attempting to reassure her. "The detective might be a back stabber, but he won't kill us."

I feel her hand sliding inside my Pharaoh Productions safari jacket.

"What are you doing?" I say, my heart skipping a beat but at the same time, my soul feeling a slow burn.

263

She steals my 9mm from out of its holster. Back-stepping, she points the business end of the piece at my face and smiles. Pressing herself up against Cipriani's bulky shoulder, she exhales, and sighs.

"Chase 'Ren Man' Baker," she says, as if scolding one of her freshman English 101 students. "When will you ever learn? Naturally I knew from the start that you'd worked with Andre eight years ago on the first failed dig. How could I *not* know? It's why I chose you to locate him in the first place."

"I kept telling him his dick would get him into big trouble one day," the detective says in his smooth, low-toned Italian.

The two goons take their respective places beside me, one on each side.

"Hey, what's a dick for?" I say. "You weren't very good in the sack anyway honey."

I see Cipriani's face drop as Anya's eyes go wide.

I smile.

"Oh Cip, you didn't know? Oh, well, I'm sure your girlfriend would have gotten around to telling you the truth about our sleeping bag adventure in the desert eventually."

"Tie him up," the detective orders.

"Oh good," I say. "We're gonna play some games now."

It's the last thing I remember saying before the goon on my left balls his fist in my face.

49

In the dream *I'm floating above a cemetery. I know it's a cemetery because I can see the headstones, the mausoleums and the green, rolling, rural pastures from high up in the friendly skies. In fact, it's a cemetery that I know from a long time ago. The three-hundred-year-old Albany Rural Cemetery. The same cemetery that I would sneak into at night back when I was kid when and I would go in search of buried treasures with my* Radio Shack *metal detector. Most people don't know it, but old cemeteries are ripe with all sorts of artifacts from hundreds of years back. Old belt buckles, coins, even musket balls took a special place of honor on my childhood bookshelves.*

Soon I begin to fall.

Not rapidly as first, but slowly, gently. The closer I come to the earth, the more a single burial plot captures my attention. It's an ornate plot that is made up of a square granite stone. Set where a headstone should be is a cross. A massive cross, I should say, maybe twenty feet high, its cross beam no less than seven feet in diameter. The cross is fashioned in the traditional manner of the Knights Templar, with half-moon-shaped edges. A Maltese cross. Situated before the cross and directly behind the stone, is a life-sized statue of a woman. A woman veiled in flowing robes, her hands hanging down at her sides, her eyes raised to the heavens. She is not the Virgin Mary, but she is somebody else entirely. Only, I can't exactly tell who she is. Not yet. I'm too far up in the sky to know for certain.

But then something happens.

I stall, and I feel myself begin to drop. Hard, like a rock.

I see the cross and the face of the stone woman coming at me fast, see her mouth opening up, the lids on her eyes raising up, see the blood pouring out of them and down onto her cheeks...

And then I'm awake, the bright sun now shining directly into the open window above the table, stinging my eyes.

"Good to have you back with us, Chase," Cipriani says, having tossed a glass of tap water into my face. "I wouldn't want you to miss this for the world."

One of the goons has already removed the padlock from the box and is now toying with the box's built-in lockset. He's using an electronic tool to pick the lock. The cordless tool sounds not unlike a dentist's drill. My head hurts. Bad. My vision is cloudy and a steady but loud pulse pounds in my brain. I take slow, short breaths. Try not to talk while I attempt to gather my wits back about me.

Then, a distinct click fills my ears, like metal breaking away from metal, as the lockset drops to the wood floor. There's the coppery taste of blood in my mouth that I only just noticed, and my left eye is partially closed, swollen. I tongue my front teeth. One of my molars feels loose. Did the goon continue to beat me while I was out? It's entirely possible if not probable.

"Keep your good eye on this one, Chase," Cip says, his smile glowing brighter than the Duomo's golden cupola on a sunny Tuscan afternoon.

He steps over to the box, shooing away the second goon with a carefree wave of his hand. I glance at Anya who has her hands cathedraled at the knuckles and pressed up against the underside of her chin. She's on pins and needles awaiting the true contents of the box. Behind me stands the other goon. The one who punched me out. He's teasing me by flicking my right earlobe with his sausage thick index finger. I try and shrug him off, but it only makes him do it all the more.

Cipriani approaches the box, stands before it with his back to me, blocking my view entirely. Good eye or no good eye. He uses both his hands to lift the attached lid on the strong box. Its rusted hinges squeak as he slowly lifts. When the squeaks stop, I know he's opened the lid entirely. Most of the oxygen is sucked out of the room then. An overwhelmed Anya is crying real tears. Even the goons are transfixed, the one behind me no longer flicking my earlobe.

The detective reaches in with his hands, pulls something out, sets it down onto the dining room table. It's a brown, leather bag. Large enough to fit the bones of a human being, including a skull. Or a partial skull anyway. The bag is bound together with leather shoelace-like straps. Cipriani carefully unties them, proceeds to unwrap them. When he's done, he sets the straps onto the table beside the bag. Then, inhaling a deep breath, he slowly opens the bag wide. Reaching inside with a thick, naked, trembling hand, he comes back out with something.

It's not a bone.

It's a piece of wood. A rounded piece of wood that might make up the seatback of an old harvest chair. He slaps the wood down onto the table, then reaches in again. He comes back out with another piece of wood, and another.

"What is this merda?" he barks, the desperation in his voice painfully evident.

"It's not the bones," Anya cries, lowering her hands. "After everything we went through to get them."

He dumps the out the entire contents of the bag. It's merely a pile of wood scraps and, just for laughs, the plastic head of a bald, baby doll. I can't help but thinking the doll must have been made in China. Back in the 1970s. I also can't help but smile at the sight of it all. After everything we went through, fought over, died over... the bones were never inside the Third Pyramid after all. It was all a ploy fabricated many years ago by someone, somehow, somewhere, to throw us off. To throw all of the seekers of the Jesus remains off.

My face might be so much hamburger right now, but I feel lighter than air inside.

"Man, Cip," I say. "That really sucks."

He turns, his big brown eyes alight like super pissed off *Chariots of fire*. He points an accusatory finger at me.

"You," he says. "You did this. You opened the box and took out the real bones of Jesus and replaced it with this...this...junk."

He takes a step towards me, the second goon by his side looking like Frankenstein on steroids, the goon behind me now having resumed his ear flicking. Cipriani raises up his hand, back slaps me. My head rings. My left eardrum feels like it's just exploded.

"Where did you hide the bones, Chase?"

"Don't know what you're talking about, Cippi," I mumble.

Another backhand ... More ringing in my head ... More ear flicking.

"Tell me where you've hidden the bones?" he presses.

"Take a look at the box and that old padlock on the floor. Look at that leather bag. It hasn't been opened in thirty-five years. If I had opened it, it would be obvious."

He slaps me again. Harder.

"You made it look like the box hasn't been opened in that time. You took the bones and made sure the box looked as if it hadn't been tampered with. That's what you did, but now you are going to tell me where you hid the bones of Jesus. Only I'm not going to be one to get it out of you. My associates will do the job effectively."

Ear Flicker comes around front. Second Goon takes his place beside him. Both men reach into their leather coat pockets at the same time, pull out a pair of thin leather gloves apiece. Second goon holds up an index finger, as if to say, *Wait just a second!* He heads into the kitchen where I hear him going through some of the silver wear drawers. When he comes back out, he's holding a paring knife and a wine opener.

"You gonna pop my cork with that?" I say.

Ear Flicker punches me in the mouth.

"We're going to remove your eye with it," Second Goon says in stilted, Italian-accented English.

"You only have two eyes," Cipriani says. "That means you only have two chances to tell us where you've placed the bones. I think that's fair."

"Oh goody," I say. "You boys from Sicily?"

Ear Flicker picks up the paring knife, presses the sharp business end against my throat, directly below the Adams apple. He wraps a huge, leather-gloved left hand around my forehead, presses the back of my skull tight against his hard gut. Using his index finger and thumb, he forces my right eyelid open. Second Goon picks up the wine opener, aims the sharp, pointed screw at my right eyeball.

"So what will it be, Chase?" Cip says, not without a smile. "Will you tell us where the bones are hidden? Or will you lose an eye for Jesus Christ?"

He belly laughs.

Ear Flicker tightens his grip.

Second Goon comes within a half inch of my eye with the screw tip.

Anya shrieks, covers her eyes with her hands.

"Hold him very still," Second Goon says. "I want to feel the pop of his eyeball when I pierce it."

The screw comes closer … Closer still …

Forgive them God, for they know not what they do.

50

It's all going in slow motion. The screw approaching my eye. The deep, guttural laughs emerging from two hundred pounds of back-stabbing Detective Cipriani. It's like a video played at slower than slow speed. I pray to the good Lord, if it's possible for the good Lord to hear me, *Please make me pass out. Pass. Out. Now!*

But it doesn't happen.

I maintain total consciousness.

At the same time, I'm trying to lift my right foot up and down in order to take advantage of an exposed nail that's embedded into the old chair's lower right leg. Trying to do it unnoticeably. If I lift and lower my foot, the duct tape wrapped around my ankle scrapes against the nail. I can feel it tearing just a tiny bit with each up-and-down movement.

I see the needle-like corkscrew about to enter into my eyeball. Funny what you recall during moments like these. Like when I was in high school and a friend of mine fell face forward on his ski pole during the Friday night ski club outing. It went directly into his right eye. He didn't lose the eye but he sported quite the shiner for the next month. All the while he kept insisting that as bad as the injury looked, he felt no real pain, other than what came from the socket and the eyelids. I asked him how it was that he couldn't feel any pain from a ski pole being rammed into his eye. He shook his head and said, "The eyeball feels no pain. Simple as that."

As the corkscrew approaches I look forward to feeling no pain even if I am about to be half blinded.

Then, on the window sill, something appears.

Something soft, cuddly and wonderful.

I try and raise my right arm as if to shout, *Stop the corkscrew!*

"Hold it," Cipriani barks. "Looks like our raggazzo wants to talk after all."

Second Goon sports an almost disappointed look on his clean-shaven mug as he steps away with the corkscrew. Ear Flicker removes his hand from my face allowing me to close my eyelids around the now dry eyeball. I try and focus the other swelled eye on the window sill, on another set of eyes looking back at me. Eyes that are black and angry. Eyes that belong to a face sporting exposed white fangs.

"So then, Chase," Cipriani says, "what do you have to say for yourself?"

"This is what I have to say, Cippi: Sick 'em, Lu!"

51

It's a beautiful scene really. Nature's grace
incarnate. The two year old female pit bull leaping
from off the window sill directly onto the face of
Detective Cipriani, her front fangs impaling
themselves into his bulbous nose, her claws tearing
at his eyes, the two goons desperately trying to
remove the dog but Lulu biting them in the hands
shredding their leather gloves.

I give my right leg one final hard thrust upwards
against the nail, and the duct tape tears away.
Immediately, I swing the now freed booted foot up
into the crotch of Second Goon, dropping him on
the spot. Then, lifting myself up, I manage to stand
on the same free leg but, at the same time, bent
forward as if bowing for an audience, the chair legs
pointing out and away from my backside like the
horns on a bull. In that manner I back-step quickly,

rushing Ear Flicker with my bull horns. I slam into him, pinning him against the wall, the hardwood chair legs gouging his stomach and ribs. He screams and falls to the floor like a sack of rags and bones.

Then comes a shot, followed by two more shots.

Lifting my head I make out a tiny spatter of blood that stains Anya's right cheek. She drops to the floor beside the now lifeless Second Goon. Meanwhile, the brick walls rattle with Cipriani's tortured screams as Lu continues to bury her powerful jaws into his bearded face.

Until I shout, "Lu! Basso!"

The dog immediately obeys and releases the crooked cop. Coming to me, she jumps up on my legs, tries to lick my face with her blood-stained teeth, lips, and tongue.

Now coming through the open window is a man with a smoking gun in his hand.

Checco.

"Took you so long?" I say.

"I took Lu to the pet spa to have a wash and a nail clipping." Now looking around the room. "Mamma mia, what kind of mess did you step into here?" Then, his eyes back on me and where I'm once more seated, still duct-taped to the chair. "Wait, Chase, don't answer that. Not yet anyway."

"Can you un-tape me, please?"

"Of course," he says. Then, "You'll be needing some emergency house cleaning, I can see. Shall I add it to my bill?"

"I still owe you for cleaning up after that Vatican soldier I left bleeding on my floor a few days ago."

He shakes his head.

"Ah yes, I meant to speak with you about that. When my people arrived, they expected to find a dead man along with lots of blood. They were prepared naturally, for the worst. But, instead, the man you shot in the leg was gone. Disappeared. And your apartment was clean. No blood. No sign of violence."

He must have survived, I think. The Vatican soldier must have survived the shooting. Or, at the very least, his own people came and got him. Then they cleaned up all the evidence. Why they would bother at that point, I have no idea. Better not to think about that for now.

"Search the girl," I say, as he cuts away the tape from my wrists. "Let's hope she's got cash, or at least an American Express that's not maxed out."

"Yes," he says. "Lucky for you I am proud to take American Express for my services."

52

As promised Checco has the entire placed cleaned of bodies and blood. Checco, an expert shot, knew precisely where to shoot Anya so that she wouldn't die or, for that matter, receive an injury that would require years of healing. He did however, put a .22 caliber round in her right shoulder, which necessitated the services of an EMT van. He wasn't so kind with the goons, having put them permanently out of the bullying and torture business. The damage Lu did to Cipriani's face required a second EMT van. The wounds are more emotional than physical (the face bleeds a lot, after all). But no doubt they will also require the services of a very decent plastic surgeon. I hope someone can recommend a good one for Cip while he resides in prison for the rest of his days.

But then, it's more likely that Detective Cipriani

won't go to prison. In fact, it's more probable the crooked cop will find someplace quiet to retire while his wounds heal. Not the wounds from his face, but the wounds to his financial hopes and dreams now that he knows the bones of Jesus will not be his for auctioning to the highest bidder on the illegal antiquities black market.

When the bodies are gone, Checco sends a couple of associates to the Hotel Rex on the Via Faenza in order to dig through Anya's things. It's not long before he comes up with a bundle of cash and even the promised Amex. The money covers all his expenses and mine. I take only what I require for having found Dr. Manion, but no more. After all, he died on my watch. I take nothing for having gone after the bones. The bones were never mine in the first place. They are no one's. No one belonging to this earthly world anyway. In the end, it wasn't the bones I wanted, so much as the experience of going after the bones. I'm a writer now, not a sandhog. Writers require experience. And what an experience it's been searching for my maker.

"You have the money you need to go home now, Chase," Checco says, running his hand through his wavy black hair. He smiles at me like an innocent boy, the kind of international fixer who can arm a small revolutionary army within twenty-four hours, if the price is right. "I will take care of your child support problem and make sure you are up to date and no longer face the possibility of arrest upon your arrival in the U.S." He smiles. "Which, of course, begs the question, would you like me to book you a first class ticket to New York City?"

Checco talks. I hear him talking, and I understand what he's saying, but I can't take my eyes off the strongbox. In my head, I'm seeing the bones it was supposed to possess. I wonder if one of the scientists who was entrusted to bury the bones inside the pyramid came back for them at a later date. Maybe the bones occupy a place of honor in some private antiquity collector's personal museum. Or perhaps the Vatican secretly possesses them. But then, why send one of their soldier's after me with threats of retribution? Threats of death? Why not just let me go about my business knowing I would never find the bones anyway?

I feel that familiar tingling in my gut. It tells me my search for the bones of my maker is not yet finished. Just as well. All novels, good or bad, need a proper ending.

A hand waved in my face.

"Earth to Chase," Checco sings. "Shall I purchase you a ticket?"

He breaks me out of my spell.

"Yes, Checco," I say. "Yes, that would be great."

He slips into his windbreaker.

"Will that be round-trip or one-way?" he adds, while making his way across the dining room and the living room to the front door.

I turn and look at him. Into his face.

"What do you suggest?" I say.

He shrugs his shoulders.

"I think we both know that eventually, Cipriani is going to come after you again. He and his Sicilian ragazzi."

I nod. Checco is right. I'm not the type to run

from trouble. But then, who wants to be constantly looking over his shoulder?

"Make it one-way," I say.

"Good choice. I'll text you when the reservation is made. It will of course be an electronic ticket."

He opens the door.

"Checco?" I call out.

"Yes?"

"Will I ever see you again?"

"In a few months," he says. "I come to New York. You can take me to the Empire State Building."

"Deal."

"Enjoy your daughter, Chase."

"Thank you."

He steps out, closing the door behind him.

Which leaves me all alone with an empty strongbox that was recovered from a secret chamber inside the Third Pyramid. While Lu lies on the couch, trying to catch some much needed Zs, I feel a sudden wave of sleepiness wash over me. Maybe that's because, other than catching a quick nap or two on the fishing boat from Alexandria to Italy, I haven't slept in forty-eight hours.

In the bathroom I wash my face, remove the dried blood from around my mouth, apply some antibiotic ointment to my fat lower lip. I feel around the inside of my mouth with my index finger, pushing and pulling on my teeth, especially on what I thought was a loose molar. Every tooth is both present and accounted for and solidly in place. Chase the lucky dog.

From the bathroom I make my way into the

kitchen, find an already opened bottle of whiskey, pour myself a tall shot. Taking it back out into the dining room with me, I set it out onto the table beside the empty strongbox. I dig into my left trouser pocket, empty it out. There's a little cash which consists of Euros and useless Egyptian pounds. Some coins, some small rocks and sand that found its way into my pockets along the way. I empty my back pockets of my wallet and passport, then I remove whatever is still stuffed into my right trouser pocket.

That's when I see it again.

The cross I pulled off the Vatican soldier.

The Maltese cross which contains the statuette of a robed woman at its base. I feel a cold shiver run up and down my spine. I dreamt about this cross when I was passed out from the beating the goon was giving me. I dreamt I was flying over a cemetery I knew from my youth. Why would I dream of this cross if it weren't speaking to me? Calling me?

The job of finding your maker is not finished...

I lift the glass off the table, take a deep drink, set it back down. Then I pick it up the cross by its leather strap, stare at it. Stare at the woman. For a brief second I almost feel like the miniature statue is staring back at me. Communicating with me.

I turn the cross over. That's when I see the small inscription.

Double-timing it to my bedroom, I find my reading glasses, take them back out to the dining room with me. In the light from the still open window, I read the inscription.

Erastus
Section 24, Lot 8
GPS coordinates: 42.7076416, -73.7338181

There's that name again ... Erastus. The same name uttered by the Vatican soldier before he fainted on my apartment floor from blood loss.

Who or what the hell is Erastus?

What is section 24? Lot 8? Sounds almost like a parcel of land. But then, with the GPS coordinates that are also provided, it must be a plot of land. But where?

About-facing, I open my laptop, boot it up.

When it's ready I type in Google Maps. With hands that are almost to the point of trembling, I type in the GPS coordinates into the designated boxes, then come down on the Enter key with my index finger.

The location that comes up takes my breath away.

It's as if this entire journey were leading me to this very place on earth. After all the running I've been doing, the chasing, the digging, the disappearing, I am finally going back to the one place on earth I can never truly escape.

I am going home again.

Going home to meet my maker.

53

The flight arrives in New York's JFK at 7:07 in the morning.

Fifteen minutes early thanks to a lighter than usual headwind, or so the captain politely informs us.

I have a choice here. I can immediately head into the city and surprise my ex-wife and daughter now, or I can head upstate to finish the job I started days ago. Truth is, there never was a choice. I want to see my daughter more than anything in the world. But I know that I cannot be hers entirely. Not until I nail the lid shut on this mystery ... This chase.

That in mind, I take a cab into the city and hop a train for Albany at Penn Station.

All during the train ride north, my eyes staring outside onto the Hudson River as the train winds its way along the banks, I can only wonder if my instincts are going to serve me right. If the bones of Christ are to be found not in Jerusalem or Egypt, but in New York of all places, the irony would not be profound, but almost comical. If they are to be found only within a mile of my birthplace and inside a cemetery where I used to play my Indiana Jones games as a scrappy-haired kid, I will know for certain that my life will have taken a humbling turn for the surreal. Or, what the hell, maybe it will all simply be a bizarre coincidence.

I ride, careful to keep a watchful eye on my surroundings, knowing that I am not yet out of danger. That at any moment, anyone of a number of enemies can jump me when I least expect it, those enemies now including certain corrupt members of the Florence police force.

By the time the train pulls into the station in Albany, it is going on noon. Outside the station I hail a cab and immediately tell the driver to take me to the Albany Rural Cemetery.

"Who died?" the old, overweight white man says from behind the steering column.

"A very important man," I say. "Lived a long time ago."

He looks at me in the rearview with tired eyes.

"You're a little late for the funeral," he says, with a lung cracking smoker's laugh.

"Two thousand years too late," I say.

I see his eyes do a roll in their sockets, and he falls quiet. I couldn't be happier.

Driving over highway that borders the city of my youth, I open the window and take in the sweet smell of spring in upstate New York.

Albany.

The capital of the Empire State. Considered a backwater by some. A home for state workers and not much else. A place lost in time, always in the shadow of its far more popular bigger sister to the south. New York City.

How long has it been for me?

Maybe twenty years since I last laid my eyes on her tall buildings and the Hudson River that flows calm and heavy from the winter run-off in the spring. It dawns on me suddenly that I have nothing to dig with. Leaning forward, I instruct the cabbie to make a quick detour to the nearest hardware store, where I will purchase a shovel and a pickaxe. He does it. When I get back inside the cab, I lay the tools onto the floor as the cabbie questions me over what I'm about to do with the digging equipment.

"Rob a grave," I tell him.

He doesn't laugh.

As we approach the village of Menands in North Albany, I remove the cross from the pocket in my jacket. I stare down at it, at the Maltese cross and the angelic lady. At her little eyes, hands, and wings. I feel my heart beat and my lungs strain to breathe. My gut is speaking to me, telling me that he's close. The remains of Christ are very close.

The cabbie pulls up to the cemetery gates, comes to a stop under a metal sign that reads, The Albany Rural Cemetery, Incorporated April 2, 1841. I know the old metal sign well, even if it only dawns on me now that perhaps the founding cemetery fathers wanted to avoid incorporating a resting place for the dead on April Fool's Day, or what was then known as the Feast of Fools day.

"You want me to drive inside?" asks the cabbie.

I tell him it won't be necessary. Paying the man, I tip him generously and get out. As he pulls away I stare down a long avenue bordered on both sides with wide-open greens which are bookended with thick woods. Pulling out my cell phone, I go to VZ Navigator and type in the same GPS coordinates that I Google mapped prior to leaving Italy. It zeros in on a plot that can't be located more than a half mile away along the cemetery road.

Pocketing the smartphone and hefting the tools over my shoulder, I walk.

The road winds and bends until the pristine greens become covered with hundreds upon hundreds of headstones, ornate statuary, and in some cases, mausoleums that are larger than my downtown New York apartment. The Albany Rural Cemetery is not just any cemetery. It is the resting place of former U.S. President Chester Arthur, renowned architect Philip Hooker, an entire rebel brigade from the Revolutionary War, and one more important man: Erastus Corning, the mayor who presided over Albany for more than forty-one years until his death in 1978. The same year the Vatican called for the shroud inquiry. The same year the bodies from the Jesus tomb were removed from Jerusalem and supposedly, reburied inside a secret vault inside the Third Pyramid of Giza.

"Erastus ..." whispered the Vatican soldier as he lie bleeding on my apartment floor. "Erastus ... Erastus ..."

Certain he was going to die, he was telling me

the location of the bones. When I grabbed the cross strapped to his neck, he must have assumed that I was now without question, in possession of the true resting place of Jesus. If only I'd thought to read the inscription on the cross's back, so much death and destruction could have been avoided. But then, my primary purpose was to find Manion. I found him, but I could not prevent him from losing his life in pursuit of the bones. If only I'd thought to read the inscription far earlier than I did ...

I see the headstone from maybe fifty feet away. The granite Maltese cross is easy to spot amongst the tall oak and birch trees. My heart beating in my chest, I make my way to the cross like a penitent man approaching an altar from which he is about to be judged. The cross is taller than I thought. At least two stories tall, and carved into its center is the symbol that tells me I have come to the right place. It's a triangle with the small circle in the center. The same symbol I found on the shroud, and in the third pyramid.

My eyes shift downwards.

The angel of a woman who adorns its pedestal is as large as I am. Her copper body has oxidized over the years and become entirely green, like the Statue of Liberty. But her wings look thick and full and light, while her flowing robes seem as if they will blow in the breeze should it suddenly pick up. She looks into my eyes, and with her opens hands, begs me to come forward and perhaps even to accompany her to a world that is not of this earth. She's taking a step forward as is evidenced by her right knee which is rising up against her gown, and if I didn't know any better, it wouldn't surprise me at all if she suddenly took hold of my hand and began lifting me up into the heavens to greet the soul of the man who truly rests here.

The man who is said to be buried here is not Erastus Corning, as the engraved name indicates on the stone located directly below this angelic woman's feet, but instead they belong to someone else. Or perhaps, Erastus shares the grave. In any case, I set aside the pick-axe while positioning the shovel so that the vertical blade stabs the soft grass. I press my booted foot down on the blade and feel it sink into the soil.

It takes maybe five minutes of digging before the blade hits something solid. Something that feels and sounds like metal. All around me now, the wind blows. I've been so busy digging, that I never noticed the once bright blue sky which has blackened with thick, dark clouds. Off to the east towards the river, I spot a flash of lightning and a few seconds later, a deep rumble of thunder. Climbing out of the hole, I feel the first of the heavy raindrops pelt my face and the wind slapping my skin.

Setting down the shovel, I grab the pickaxe and jump back down into the hole.

I chop all around the box with the ax portion of the tool, and then set the pick into the earth beneath it. With one hard thrust of the thick wood handle, I free the box from the earth. Bending at the knees, I take the box into my arms and set it onto the grass. Climbing back out, I stand over it and simply look at it.

The storm has picked up, the wind blowing so hard the trees above me are bending. The sky is so black it's like night has settled in early over the land, while the rain pelts my head. A bolt of lightning strikes a tree not one hundred feet away, and a heavy branch falls from it onto the road. The explosive thunder steals my breath away. Looking back down at the box, I can see that it's locked, but that it will be possible to open it with one swift, and well-placed swipe of the ax.

Turning the box onto its side, I hold the ax in my hands, as if I were chopping wood. I position the blade over the center of the metal box, where the two halves join together. Sucking in a deep breath, I slowly raise the axe overhead and come down at the precise moment a jagged bolt of lightning strikes the road, thunder exploding like live artillery, making my ears ring and my head buzz.

I look down and see that the box is open.

I drop the ax and feel the rain that is soaking me. It's as if the rain is heaven sent. It's seeping into my clothing, soaking my skin and drowning my pounding heart. I feel suddenly paralyzed as though no longer in control of my movements. But that's insane. I'm merely afraid of what it is I'm about to find.

And then I hear a voice. It's coming from behind me.

"What is it you seek, Chase?"

I turn fast, entirely expecting to be confronted by an irate cemetery worker or even a police officer. But the man I face is someone else entirely. The man stands no more than a few feet away from me, dressed entirely in black, his black fedora protecting his head and face from the wind and the rain. He's using a heavy wood cane for balance, which he holds tightly in his left hand. More than anything else, I know now for certain that he is not dead ... that he did not bleed out on my apartment floor in Florence.

"I see what we all seek," I answer.

"And what is that exactly?" asks the man I shot ... The soldier of the Vatican.

"Erastus ..." he whispered while bleeding out on the floor of my apartment. "Erastus ... Erastus ..."

"The truth," I say, swallowing something dry. "Proof of the truth."

"And how will this proof change your life?"

I shake my head.

"It's not about that. The bones of Christ are an important artifact. Perhaps the most important in all mankind. They belong to all humanity and they should be exposed, resurrected, researched, protected."

"Perhaps they should be placed in a museum to gather dust?" he says. "Perhaps a placard above them should read, Here Lies Jesus of Nazareth, the man responsible for changing the world forever. Or, perhaps it should say: Here lies the body of a man who once gave people strength in their mortal lives and hope for a heavenly rest in their afterlife."

"People don't need to lose their faith just because mortal proof of Christ exists."

He cocks his head over his shoulder.

"Perhaps," he says. "But is that for you to determine? A writer who wishes only for fame?"

"I need to know. I need to know the truth. It's not fame I'm seeking. It's not money. In the end, I seek only truth."

"Then by all means, Chase Baker," he says, taking a careful limping step backward, "please be prepared to meet your maker."

I drop to my knees on the rain-soaked grass.

The penitent man ...

Grasping the box with both hands, I lift off the cover, toss it aside. Inside is a leather bag, not unlike the bag that was discovered in the box we took from the chamber in the Third Pyramid. I pull the bag open with my fingers, reach inside. My hand feels bone. The touch sends an electrical charge up into my arm. Into my brain. It shoots down my back and down my legs. My entire body feels charged.

I feel the Vatican soldier standing over me. I sense the lightning and the feel the thunder concussions, but I am in another place entirely. My lungs breathe, my heart beats, but I am not even certain that I am alive any longer. Perhaps it's possible that I have died and only now am becoming aware of it.

I pull something out.

It's a bone. A dark, almost richly blackened bone. If I had to guess, a leg bone. I pull something else out. It's a rib. Then I pull out another rib, and another. Only this rib is different from all the rest. This rib has been severed at the tip, as if something stabbed this body. Reaching in once more I pull something out that feels like rusted metal and bone fused together. It's an ankle bone. Piercing the ankle bone is a nail. But not a nail in the traditional sense. More like a spike that has blackened and rusted with time. The pointed end of the spike has been pounded with a hammer so that it now bends at a ninety-degree angle. It's a trick the Roman soldiers once employed during execution by crucifixion in order to keep the spike from slipping out of the wood once the blood began to lubricate it.

Another bolt of lightning. Another thunder explosion.

I hear something else now too. Prayers. The Vatican soldier is reciting prayers in Latin. When I glance up at him, he is not looking at the remains of Jesus. He is instead peering up at the heavens as if they are about to open up for him. I watch the rain pelt his face and I wonder if it is possible for my heart to pound any faster without exploding.

I reach in again, and this time come out with something entirely metal. It's a spear point. It's rusted and, like the spike that pierces the ankle, blackened with age, time and exposure. Can this really be the spear that pierced Christ's side? The spear of Longinus? The spear that that caused blood and water to pour forth from the wound? I set it down and reach into the bag one last time.

It's the last object in the bag and judging by the touch, it is entirely bone.

I pull out the object and stare into the eyes of Jesus. My eyes lock onto his face. His cheekbones and teeth. My eyes see the sockets where Jesus saw God the father in the kingdom of heaven. I raise myself up from my knees, hold the skull of Christ in my hands, and like the Vatican soldier, peer up at the sky and feel the rain and the wind and an unexplainable energy that radiates throughout my body.

I know the truth now. I know that the Koran is not true. Jesus did not survive the cross. He did not use a stand-in to suffer the cross in his place. He suffered the cross on his own, and he died from his sufferings ... From the scourging, the nails, the cross, the spear that pierced his side. I know now that on the third day his soul ascended into heaven leaving behind his mortal corpus. It's the truth. It must be the truth. The only truth. In my heart, I know it to be true.

There comes another bolt of lightning that strikes the earth beside me.

I never hear the thunder that follows. Only the quick click of the electrical discharge, the flash of brilliant heavenly white light and then nothing, as my world goes black.

54

I open my eyes onto the most brilliant blue sky I have ever witnessed.

Or so it seems.

I am lying on my back, on the smooth grass. The gale force wind is gone now, replaced with a gentle sweet smelling breeze. The kind of clean spring air I recall as a child when almost nothing mattered and my life was immortal. I sit up and see that almost no signs of the storm that was ravaging this cemetery only moments ago remain. There are only the trees now in full bloom, the birds singing in them, and the chirping of the crickets.

Not far from where I am seated, I see three deer feeding on the overgrown grass. To the right of them, a dozen wild turkeys collected together in a tight pack are sneaking their way around some old marble headstones, on their way to the safety of the woods.

I stand.

That's when I see that the Vatican soldier is still there. His clothing is dry, as if the rain never fell on him at all. Gripped in his left hand is his wood cane. Gripped in the other are the pick-axe and shovel handles. He's bearing a curious smile on his face.

"Did you find what you were seeking?"

I nod.

"I suppose I did," I say. "How long was I out?"

"Does it matter?"

Looking down, I can see that the hole I dug in the earth has been filled in, the sod replaced so perfectly, no one would ever know that the ground was disturbed in the first place.

I look up at the man.

"How did you ..."

But I never finish my question. I'm not sure he would answer it anyway. Maybe this ground is indeed sacred, and bears the same restorative powers of the one man on earth who was said to be resurrected on the third day.

He says, "Perhaps the time has come for you to leave this place, go home to your daughter. It's been a long time, Chase. You've been gone for too long."

He knows about my daughter ...

I glance at my watch. The time is ten past noon.

How can that be?

I shake my wrist. There's got to be a problem with the watch. But the watch is operating perfectly, like it always has. The time was eleven-fifty when the cabbie dropped me off at the cemetery. But, according to my watch, that's only twenty minutes

296

ago. It took me most of that time just to make my way on foot into the cemetery.

I peer down at the plot, at the grass, then shift my eye up to the Maltese cross, to the triangular symbol with the round hole in the center, to the bronze angelic woman who stares not at me but into me. I look at the name, Erastus Corning, embedded into the rock. I honestly can't say if I truly did uncover the bones of Christ or if I somehow dreamed the experience. Perhaps I was struck by lightning on the way into the cemetery and what followed was a bizarre journey that occurred not in upstate New York in some old cemetery, but inside my brain.

I take a step back, look over my left shoulder for the Vatican soldier.

Only he's no longer there.

I look over my opposite shoulder, and when I don't find him there either, I make a full three-hundred-sixty-degree turn, pivoting on my boot heels. He's gone, along with my digging tools. How a wounded man could simply sneak away like that without my noticing boggles my mind. But then, a lot of what has transpired this afternoon boggles my mind.

I've told you before that I'm not a praying man. But I find myself making the sign of the cross, whispering the words, "In the name of the father, and of the son, and of the holy ghost."

When it's done I whisper "Amen" aloud.

I turn and head back towards the cemetery gates, knowing in my heart that I have for certain, finally met my maker. But that he is gone again. This time, gone forever.

EPILOGUE

One Week Later

I'm holding the hand of a girl I love.

Only this girl isn't the wife of some jealous husband. She's my eight-year-old daughter. This morning I have the distinct pleasure of accompanying her on her walk to school, which isn't far from where she lives with her mother and stepfather on Gramercy Park.

She's tall for her age. She wears her brunette hair long like her mother and is very neat and fastidious about her very feminine appearance. "This is New York City after all," the ever-precocious second grader will often remind me.

She's also inherited her mother's deep-set brown eyes that used to make my heart skip a beat when I looked directly into them. Last but not at all least, she's inherited her mother's gift for gab.

"Daddy," she says, as we turn the corner onto East 22nd Street not far from the police station. "Did you really see the pyramids in Egypt?"

I squeeze her little hand.

"Yup. Went inside them too."

"Whoa. Was it scary?"

"A little."

"Did you see mummies?"

"Sort of."

"Oh my god. I would be like, really, really, REALLY scared the mummies would come alive and chase me. Like in that movie."

I laugh.

"That stuff only happens in Hollywood."

"Still gives me nightmares, dad."

"Just remember. It's all make believe."

"Like your books?"

"Yeah sure. Like my books."

We come to the school where other parents are dropping off their kids curbside and some of the teachers are waiting outside on the stone steps, greeting them as they enter the old five-story red brick public school.

Her hand slips out of mine. She turns and looks up at me with those brown eyes.

"Daddy, are you going away again? On another adventure? Or, what do you call them, research trips?"

I bend down so I can look directly at her face.

"Not for a while. I have a new book to write first."

She smiles.

300

"Oh good. Will the book have mummies in it?"

"Maybe."

"Will it have God in it?"

Her question takes me by surprise.

"Why do you ask that?"

She giggles.

"I don't know. It just came out."

"God works in mysterious ways, so they say."

"Do you believe in God, daddy?"

It's strange, because I suddenly feel my eyes welling up. I'm looking at my daughter, but in my head I'm seeing the shroud and the secret chamber inside the Third Pyramid and I'm seeing the Vatican soldier whom I shot in the leg and who later on, stood by my side while I excavated the bones of Jesus of Nazareth.

Slowly I straighten back up while reaching into my trouser pocket. I pull something out, place it over her head so that it hangs off her neck. It's the miniature cross with the angelic statuette of the woman attached to it.

"Yes, honey," I say. "I do believe in God. You can too if you want."

She takes the cross in her little fingers and looks at it with awe.

"Is this real treasure from your adventures?"

"Yup. Don't lose it."

"I'll hang on to it with all my might forever and ever." She hugs my legs so tightly I think they might break. "Thank you, daddy. Thank you."

She releases her hold, shifts her baby blue and pink peace-sign-covered backpack up on her shoulder and turns for the school stairs, where a young lady takes her hand. After issuing me a quick, pleasant smile and a wave, the young lady leads my daughter into the building. As always when my little girl leaves my sight, my throat goes tight and my heart sinks.

Walking back towards my apartment in the warmth of the morning sun, I check my smartphone for any new emails.

The top one belongs to an address I don't recognize. But the subject heading says: "ERASTUS. Not Spam." I open the email while I slowly walk along the busy sidewalk. It reads,

"Thought you might find this of interest. By the way, you still have my cross. It's okay. I want you to keep it.

"Yours in good faith.

"Pax

"Father Gabrielle"

In my head I once more picture the Vatican soldier. His dark clothing, his black fedora, the limp I gave him after I shot him in the left thigh inside my apartment vestibule. His cross now belongs to my daughter as if he somehow fully intended for her to have it.

God works in mysterious ways ...

At the bottom of his email is a hyperlink.

Stopping in my tracks on the sun-soaked sidewalk, I press the link and wait for the website to come up. It's the digital version of the *Times Union*

Newspaper. My old hometown newspaper in Albany. The piece Father Gabrielle has linked me to bears the headline, "Mayor Erastus Corning Grave Unearthed for Reburial."

Glancing at the story I can see that the resting place of the old Albany mayor was excavated on an emergency basis after flood waters from some recent severe rainstorms threatened to erode the entire burial site. While a new plot has not yet been chosen by the surviving Corning family, the remains of Mr. Corning are said to be stored in an undisclosed location.

Accompanying the story is a photo. The big monument bearing the full-sized Maltese cross and its angelic bronze lady has been removed, the ground beneath it all dug up. There's nothing left. Nothing to indicate that a body was ever buried there, much less the mortal remains of Jesus.

I find myself smiling, laughing.

So I didn't imagine seeing Jesus after all. And naturally, my having tracked down the true bones of Christ did not go unnoticed by the Vatican and those who shall remain anonymous but who bear most of the power in this world. The political and religious leaders. The spinners and the puppeteers ... The cave painters ... Those men and women who, through the centuries, have created the things we believe in and the rules we live and die by. The things that give us hope, true or false ... The things that give meaning to our mortal lives.

Pocketing the smartphone, I resume my walk back to my studio apartment above the Italian restaurant. It's time to get to work on my new novel.

THE END

*If you enjoyed **The Shroud Key**, you might also enjoy the second novel in the **Chase Baker Thriller** series, **Chase Baker and the Golden Condor.***

ABOUT THE AUTHOR

Vincent Zandri is the *New York Times* and *USA Today* best-selling author of more than sixteen novels, including *The Innocent, Godchild, The Remains, Moonlight Falls,* and *The Shroud Key.* A freelance photojournalist and traveler, he is also the author of the blog *The Vincent Zandri Vox.* He lives in New York and Florence, Italy. For more, go to www.vincentzandri.com.

Made in the USA
Columbia, SC
30 October 2023

25125168R00172